OUT OF BODY

OUT OF BODY

FIRST EDITION

A Boner Book by
The Nazca Plains Corporation
Las Vegas, Nevada
2006

ISBN:1-887895-28-0

Published by,

The Nazca Plains Corporation ®
4640 Paradise Rd, Suite 141
Las Vegas NV 89109-8000

PUBLISHER'S NOTE
Out of Body is a work of fiction created wholly by the author's
imagination. All characters are fictional and any resemblance
to any persons living or deceased is purely by accident. No
portion of this book reflects any real person or events.

Cover Model Travis Jay
Editor, Blake Stephens
Cover Art and Photo by Corwin
Art Direction, Robert Steele

Dedication

This book is dedicated to the men in my life: Steve (Teewee), Billy, Wayne, Jimmy, Casey, Craig, Ricky and course David and Chuck, with thoughts of all the others who have crossed my path. A part of each of you has been imprinted on my life.

From the author

The story of how I came to write *Out of Body* is interesting in and of itself. Perhaps I'll tell you about it in the sequel. I will say that the book was written before I went looking for a publisher. I chose to bring my novel to The Nazca Plains Corporation because I've known them for sometime.

During a phone conversation I told the publisher that I'd written a novel. He asked only question; what was it about? When I told him it was the story of a man who woke up each morning with a different boyfriend he replied, "Oh, then it's the story of your life."

In retrospect I'll admit that I have had several boyfriends during my life. Some have lasted a year, some several. And, while none of the men in our hero Chadwick White's life have been in mine, small aspects of each have contributed to this story. Still, to those of you who ask, I am not Chadwick. He has a life of his own.

Many years ago a friend was describing his wife to me. He told me that someone else might see her as an older woman but when he looked at her he saw the young woman he married, the glow of motherhood from when his children were born, the caring face which stared down at him after his heart attack and the lovely smile that made him want to fight to stay alive. In short, he explained, he couldn't see his wife like a snapshot but rather as a timeline containing all of the images he'd stored over their lifetime together.

To that end, and despite what I wrote just two paragraphs ago, Chadwick's story and my own are quite similar. Again, and for legal purposes, none of my varied boyfriends are depicted in this book. At the same time, I can honestly say that the man I am today reflects the many lives I've lived and the variety of boyfriends I've known through a long life.

If you look at your own lives I will bet you can relate. I think we all can say that every boyfriend or close friend or acquaintance that has crossed our paths has left something of themselves imprinted on our personalities. That is to say, the person you are today is not simply a snapshot but a life continuum of experiences and relationships.

In my case, my many lives have been a blessing. I've not only known a variety of boyfriends, but also a variety of lifestyles and professions. When I met my first lover as a young man, we knew nothing about "being gay", we were simply in love. We were students and our life together reflected the mentality and interests of students. I found the gay community and my second boyfriend simultaneously. Together we discovered the activism which survives in me today. In many ways that boyfriend was my soul mate. Though he is no longer alive, I love him still.

Boyfriend three was a conservative Christian. Number four believed in Western Magik. Indeed, each of the men I've lived with and loved has been totally unique. My career path has been equally as diverse. I was a police officer before becoming an attorney; I entered politics and began to write. I've been a bartender and a videographer and an artist. Finally, in what proved to be the most important of my many professions, eleven years ago I became a parent.

For those of you , who feel you can not relate to my strange life, let me remind you that you too have had many lives. In the most simple of terms, you've been a child, then a teenager and now an adult. At one time you were the son or daughter of your parents but now have transformed into your own person. You may have had many professions or at the very least many life experiences. When you look in the mirror you no doubt see all of these people and all of these lives as one. It is your life, and in some ways it may resemble my life if not Chadwick's.

If I were to come up with a single statement to sum up my many lives and make sense of my very diverse time on Earth it would be something that boyfriend number four taught me. He was the boyfriend who believed in Magik. Among the many things he taught me was to "experience the ordinary in an un-ordinary way". I realized when he gave me that advice that I had been unknowingly following it all along. Since then, I've made an effort to follow his advice consciously.

One of my favorite quotes comes from *Auntie Mame*. "Life if a banquet, and most poor suckers are starving to death," Mame tells her young charge, Patrick.

These then are the two things I tell you. Don't starve! Experience the banquet and experience it in an un-ordinary way.

Like my own experience, Chadwick White has been unknowingly following those two pieces of advice throughout this first book. In the sequel which I'm writing now, he comes to understand all that such advice means. Whether or not you ever read that next book in Chadwick's saga, try to answer the question he leaves with you at the end of this book. What would you do if you woke up each morning with a different boyfriend?

Thank you for reading my novel!

Ron Ehemann

OUT OF BODY

FIRST EDITION

A Novel by
Ron Ehemann
© Copyright 2006

A Boner Book

PROLOGUE

Did you ever have one of those mornings? You know, where you don't know if you've gotten any sleep. And you don't know if you're fully awake. And you don't know who's beside you in the bed?

Don't get me wrong... I know he's my boyfriend. I just don't know which boyfriend. And, I don't know that I want to get up and find out.

A Boner Book

CHAPTER ONE
Monday

The digital clock on my Proctor and Gamble automatic coffee maker flipped to 06:00.00. A dribble of thick black goo dropped down into the glass pot. In seconds a stream of steaming hot liquid caffeine followed suit. Upstairs, in my bedroom, at precisely the same time, my alarm went off, jolting my eyes open and my consciousness back to reality, whatever that reality was.

I hate those first few seconds when you wake up. My head hurts, my eyes burn and my brain is foggy. I blink. I blink again. I blink a third time and throw the sheet off my naked body. It's wet with my sweat and I relish the cool air as it dries my skin.

Careful not to move my body, I twist my neck and turn my head to the right. I blink again. As expected, a body-sized lump of blankets lays half a bed away. It rises and falls in a breath like rhythm betraying the fact that life exists beneath. Oh God, I think, it's my boyfriend.

Careful not to disturb his slumber I slip my legs over the edge of the mattress and slide my body smoothly from the bed. Standing, I blink again and begin to peruse the room. A single thought fills my brain. We're rich.

Real wealth can't be created. Oh you can buy a lot of expensive things, but without the experience of having lived a wealthy life, things alone won't make you wealthy. You can fill your life with expensive things, even tasteful things, but you can't buy real wealth.

Now, as I looked around the room, our room, I made mental note of the expensive things I saw.

There were crystal based lamps perched on mahogany night-stands to either side of the huge king sized bed. An oriental print screen stood hiding the matching mahogany dressing table across the more than impressively large room. On the floor, near the foot of the bed, a silk sheet lay crumpled. It had to have a six hundred thread count, and it was monogrammed. Lying on top of the sheet, almost hidden in its folds, was an empty Waterford crystal goblet. A bottle of Dom Perion lay next to it, spilt and staining the sheet. I found another empty bottle on the floor in front of the nightstand and a third near the foot of the bed. These two were lesser brands, though still expensive.

"Damn, we must have been drinking last night," I thought to myself as I began to shuffle across the rich oriental carpeting which covered that impressively large floor. I find myself headed for the bathroom, its place and purpose betrayed by Italian marble tiles. It's time for me to get ready to go to work. In route to the bathroom my eyes take in more detail, which I stash away. In the safety of the shower I'll sort them out and begin the thought process which will, hopefully, give me the edge I'll need when I return to face the man now sleeping in "our bed".

I spy with my little eye; in the corner sits a wingback chair upholstered in cream colored silk with an embossed oriental pattern. Across the chair lies the crumpled clothing that one of us had discarded before climbing into bed. Blocking my path I find a pair of Italian loafers. I kick them under the oriental chair and note how soft the leather feels on my bare feet.

"Hmm," I think to myself, "we have taste in addition to money." Despite how dim the light was, something sitting on top of the bureau glistened and caught my attention; jewelry no doubt. There was a small pile of the stuff. I didn't bother to walk over to see what was there. Not necessary. My goal was the shower.

In contrast with the drape drawn bedroom, the bathroom is bright. In similarity, the room is impressively large. The tiles beneath my feet are cool and help to bring me to a full state of consciousness. Like the bedroom, everything in the bath says wealth. Gleaming porcelain is accented with gold fixtures, the linens are crisp and appear pressed, and their monograms match the sheet back in the bedroom. Lifting the heavy Turkish terry-cloth I examine those initials - M.T.M. I chuckle. Perhaps I'm married to Mary Tyler Moore.

The shower is almost as large as the bathroom itself. It's made of a lighter colored marble, which complements the floor tiles. Stepping inside, I gently pull the faucet knob toward me and instinctively twist it to the right. I like my shower hot and steamy, much like my men.

Warm water sprays my body. Within seconds the temperature starts rising and soon my desires are fulfilled. The water has grown hot and steam starts building in the stall. The water stings my chest. What bliss. In addition to hot steamy water, I love great water pressure. My hand reaches for the bar of soap and brings it to my nose. I inhale the luscious fragrance of lavender and savor the sensation before whipping up a handful of lather. When it comes to showers I have many loves. Good soap is on the list.

Slowly I slide my hands across my skin, letting the suds caress me and clean away the sins of last night. It wouldn't do for me to arrive at work smelling of sex or sleep or stale champagne, even if it were good champagne.

I can literally feel my muscles relax under the relenting massage of the water. The steam begins to fog the glass door separating me from my life out there, with what's-his-name. The steam clouds the glass, and as I expected, my mind begins to clear.

For me, remembering is a visual thing. First images begin to flash in my mind. There's a face. There's a place. Now there are more people and more places and situations beginning to present themselves. Like snapshots, which no one ever bothered to label or sort, the imagery is disjointed and confusing when it first begins. But as the pile of imaginary photographs grows larger the randomness begins to subside and an order, of sorts, emerges. The rise of order brings the flashes faster and faster and faster until, like a silent movie, a jerky movement begins to emerge. This morning, here in the shower, the images begin. At first flash I'm startled. Then, reminded of how it begins every morning, I allow myself to relax and let the imagery flow. Soon, I am drawn into the movie.

There I am, one of the main characters. I don't even look at the other characters, not yet.

I've found it better not to try sorting the people. Just like the first flashes of imagery, if you let the characters pile up they'll start to sort themselves. Rather, I focus on the background details. Sooner or later I'll start to recognize the setting or situation and absorb the rest of the story.

This morning as the movie in my mind unfolds it is the house or apartment which I recognize first. Funny, but it isn't the crystal based lamps or the mahogany bedroom suite or really anything I've run into between the bed and the bath that I recognize. It is the look and feel of the place itself. Like everything else, it reeks of old wealth and superb taste. Down to the detail, nothing has been overlooked and nothing left to chance.

Like the bedroom, all of the rooms are large, really large. They are filled with expensive furnishings and generously sprinkled with antiques. Artwork is everywhere and includes both framed pieces as well as sculpture.

I'm standing there, looking at a painting. There are people all around, lots of people, and they're dressed to the nines. Most of them have cocktails in their hands. Clearly, it's a party. The painting that has my attention is beautiful.

In it, a young woman in a long green dress lies prone on the grass. Behind her a tree and in her hand she holds an apple. At her side a young child sits staring into the woman's eyes. The child has the woman's total attention. She had my total attention too. I was mesmerized.

The expression on her face is peaceful and adoring, not unlike the Madonna's of a million paintings in Rome. I stare at the woman's face, her beautifully loving face. I am mesmerized.

"It's called Temptation by William Bouguereau", says a deep baritone voice.

Startled, I turned to identify the source of that knowledge. He is tall, dark and to complete the cliché, handsome. Jet-black hair of medium length dips low to his brows though not so low as to cover his steel blue eyes. Sharply defined angles accent his face. I am still mesmerized though my attention has shifted from the painting to the man. I find myself staring at his face, equally as mesmerized as I had been with the face in the painting. His blue eyes become liquid and alive. I am drawn into them. Suddenly small lines form to either side of those eyes and he breaks into a wide, brilliantly white smile. I catch my breath.

I remained mute a bit longer than I wanted, no doubt giving him the impression that I was dumb-struck by his appearance, but he took it in stride.

"Bouguereau painted through the turn of the century," he continued. "He's one of the Pre-Raphaelites. Temptation was one of his many Biblical works. Do you like it?"

"Yes", I admitted. I did like the painting, and I liked this dark stranger too.

"Have you seen the other art," he asked?

"Ahh..." I glanced around the room. It was filled with art. Oils and sculptures were everywhere. A huge tapestry dominated one wall, the carpet under our feet, even the furniture were works of art.

"No, I've just gotten here and haven't really had the chance to look around."

He took my arm and broke into another one of his soon to become signature smiles. Giving me a slight squeeze he winked. "Well then, let me show you around."

For the next fifty minutes or so we glided through the rooms which dominated the first level of what I learned was a massive home - well, Embassy really. It turned out that the home as well as the artwork it contained were the property of the Principality of Andorra, an obscure city-state situated between France and Spain. I'd never heard of Andorra before and I'd never heard of most of the artists whose talents were spread throughout this mansion. My host had. Room by room he deftly parted the scores of other guests to reveal yet another masterpiece to my eyes. With the expertise of a museum guide, he exposed them to my consciousness as well.

It turned out that the party was a celebration in honor of the newly appointed ambassador and that the guest list read like a Who's Who of the city's elite. In deed I was probably the only person who didn't belong there based on social status alone. As my host described the art, he described the other guests as well. This one was the president of some corporation I'd never heard of, that one was the wife of some politician I'd only heard of, and those two across the room were the founders and largest donors of some charity organization of which everyone's heard.

Each guest was elegantly dressed. All of the women and many of the men were draped in jewelry. Our tour stopped now and then when one of the those other guests demanded a few words with my host, or when he scooped a couple of champagne flutes off the tray of a passing waiter. He handled both chores with such skill. My glass was never empty and no guest was ignored. If he lacked in any grace it was only in his failure to introduce me to those guests interrupting our artistic mission, and even then he could be excused. For one thing he didn't as yet really know me. We hadn't even exchanged names. For another, the other guests really didn't interrupt us.

"Lovely." "Charmed." "So happy to see you." Though he said very little, that huge smile overwhelmed each of our interrupters and eased what might otherwise have seemed like a social slight for he quickly turned his attention away from them and back to me.

When we had covered the width and breath of the party,

when we finished in our appreciation of each piece of art, when the third or fourth or perhaps fifth flute of bubbly had been consumed he leaned close to my ear and whispered, "Would you like to get away from here? We could go somewhere more private."

I blushed and a blinding flash of bright white light exploded in my head.

Wet, hot, steamy streams of jet fast water stung my face and snapped me back from that party. Once again I found myself standing amid the marble and gold and fog of my morning shower. The glitz and glamour of the party was now a rapidly fading memory.

Extending my arm in a circular motion I wiped some of the steam off the shower door and bent my face close to the glass. Peering out of my water cocoon through to the bedroom beyond, I confirmed that he laid there still, my lover. He was shrouded in the sheets and bedclothes which moments earlier had held us both. The steady rise and fall of his breathing brought me assurance. I turned back to my shower.

Content in the knowledge that I was still alone I forced my attention and directed my consciousness back to the embassy party. I may never know how it happens, or why, but I know how to trigger and make it happen. It's easy; all I do is let the shower wash everything else away. Concentrating only on the shower, its temperature, its force, the steam it creates around me; the rest of the world fades. At first it feels like I'm passing out. Then, as suddenly as it disappeared a moment or two earlier, the party reapears, or rather I reappear at the party. It's all so difficult to explain, you'll just have to trust me when I say that it happens and right now it has. Once again, with a flash of brilliant light, I am in the presence of that beautiful stranger.

"So," he inquires, "shall we sneak out of here and find someplace quiet?"

"Leave with you? I'm sorry," I stammered trying to hide the blush of my now red cheeks. "I don't even know you."

His arm, which I realized had been draped across my shoulder during most of the artistic tour, now slipped to my side. He took my hand in his and, looking me directly in the eyes - his own dark blue piercing stare unblinking - he raised my hand and kissed it. "Then let me introduce myself. I am Vincent d'Aguardo, and I am very pleased to meet you."

It was probably the fact that those eyes locked on mine, but when he proclaimed how very pleased he was to meet me it didn't sound or feel the same as when he'd said it to any of the other guests and interrupters. When he said those words to me they sounded genuine, a fact no doubt I betrayed by another blush. How the fuck did he get so charming, I thought? And how the fuck did he know I'd be interested? For that fucking matter, how did he even know I was gay?

I must have remained mute because he needed to prompt me to reciprocate, "I suppose I could peruse the guest list but it would be easier if you'd just tell me your name." He punctuated his prompt with another one of his disarming smiles.

Within moments I'd told him my name, Chadwick White. I told him that he probably wouldn't find me on the guest list as I was really a guest of a guest. I told him that I didn't often attend these types of parties and, I told him I'd love to go somewhere private with him. I'm surprised I didn't tell him my social security or driver's license numbers, or my blood type

As we crossed the room toward the foyer he took my arm, gently pushing it into the crook of his own. "I've never really enjoyed these parties or these people," he whispered as he deftly glided me past the mix of newcomers and late arrivals that now mingled near the door. The foyer was rather small compared to the other rooms we'd been in, and the crush of people forced us to stop.

He let go of my arm. Turning to aim his steel blue eyes at me again he flashed that smile of his again. "So, Chadwick White, do you have any questions of me?"

I thought a second. "Why yes - yes I do. Why is it you know so much about the art in this place?"

His smile grew larger and a twinkle entered those eyes. "Because," he confessed, "it is all my art."

I blinked and in the very instant of that blink another explosion of light filled my head. Once again I found myself back in my morning shower. I was frozen there unable to move. Jets of water stung my naked chest. I blinked again but I was still there, alone in my marble tomb. "Go back," I told myself, "Go back to the party and find out what he meant." I blinked again only to find myself still alone and wet. I tried to remember what to do, how to move from here. I felt my brow wrinkle. "At least some part of my body was still responding."

This time I didn't wipe the steam off the shower door. Nor did I look to confirm his presence out there in our bed. This time, more than anything, I wanted to confirm his identity and to do that I must return to the party. "Think!"

I reached forward and, grasping the handle of the shower's faucet, I twisted it sharply left. Instantly the sting of water turned measurably hotter. As I let loose of the faucet and straightened my back some of the now almost scalding spray splashed up and into my eyes. Instantly my hands were at my face, protecting it. Instinct had already closed my eyes and I began to rub them through their lids. When I again opened them my vision was momentarily blurry but as they focused the sear of hot water against my naked flesh subsided. This time there was no blinding burst of light, nothing to mark precisely when the shift occurred. I simply opened my eyes and once again I was at the party, once again I was in his presence. He was staring and smiling and holding my arm. We were alone in the crowded foyer.

"You're art?" I asked with suspicion. "I thought you told me that everything belonged to some country."

That smile again.

"I did. And, it does. You see, I am the new ambassador, this party is for me."

I did my best to keep my eyes open and trained only on him. I feared that one blink would send me back to the shower and its scalding sting. "You're the ambassador," I said, the shock no doubt showing in my voice as well as my face. "How can you be the ambassador? You only look to be twenty-one or two," I said.

He laughed.

"I'm twenty-three, and I assure you I am the new ambassador."

Looking back toward the crowded rooms behind us I blinked and tried my best to wipe the look of astonishment from my face. "I don't understand."

"What part don't you understand, my age or my appoint-ment?" He laughed again but that smile never left his face.

"Well," I stammered, "I just figured you for one of the guests, not the object of these festivities. How did you get to be the ambassador?"

A break in the crowd nearest the door afforded an opportunity to escape and he deftly guided me around a rather large lady in a fur cape and onto the front porch. "My family is very well connected. My father was one of our King's closest advisors prior to his death last year. My appointment was polit-ical, besides there are no age prerequisites to ambassador-ship."

A thought crossed my mind. "Hey, how can we leave if the party is for you?"

"It's my party, I can do what ever I want, and I want to get away... with you."

We walked down the steps and out to the curb. A man in a dark blue uniform stepped from one of the largest limou-sines I've ever seen and opened the passenger door. "Good evening sir," he said with a quick bow. "Will you be going somewhere?"

"Thanks all the same James, but I think we'll walk. The night is beautiful and I'm sure we'll be just fine. Wait for us. I've got my cell phone and if we get tired I'll call for you to pick us up."

Taking my arm in his once more, we began our stroll.

He was correct. The night was beautiful. The moon was full and bright and a faint fragrance of fall was in the air.

The embassy sat on top of a small hill and the street leading from it ran down to a river about a block away. We now walked toward that river. On either side of us the street was flanked by huge houses, perhaps even other embassies for all I knew. They were mansions as large as or larger than the one we'd just left.

Huge elm trees grew in the parkway between the street and the sidewalk upon which we were traveling. The branches of these stately trees curved upward and out into the dark of night. Antique globe streetlights cast pools of yellow illumination that served to accent the leaves. As we stepped from the sidewalk to the street, I saw that the outward curved branches of the elms from our side of the pavement reached up to meet the outward curved branches of the elms from the other side of the street. They met in a pointed arch some twenty or thirty feet up, in the center of the street, covering it completely. The effect was to create a leafy and lofty arch all the way down to the river.

The night, this street, the man whose arm was now linked with mine again - who drew me closer as we strolled along - all of these things could easily be described as a dream.

"Let this be him," I remember thinking. And, with that simple thought I was suddenly back in the marble shower. "Damn!" I wished I could quit doing that. The glass door was now completely fogged and the stall filled with steam. Not even the spray of the shower disturbed the hot cloud of vapors that enveloped me. Again I didn't bother to wipe the glass nor peer out into the bathroom or through to the bedroom. I took for granted that my boyfriend was still buried beneath that pile of sheets and blankets on the mahogany bed I'd left a short while ago. Now, more than anything, I just wanted to hide in my foggy cloud of steam and let it transport me back to that dreamy street outside the embassy, let it float me back to the arm of the handsome stranger I hopped I'd eventually find huddled in the pile on that bed.

I didn't snap back as easily as I'd hopped this time. I felt dizzy, and a lot of disjointed imagery seemed to crash into itself deep in my subconscious. There were scenes of other parties and of large functions filled with people in formal dress. I saw scenes of the tall, dark and handsome Ambassador at dinners, State dinners I'd guess from the tuxedos that he and the fifty or sixty other guests were wearing. His table was on the dais and I was always sitting at his side. I also saw images of us traveling together. Visits to his country? There were parades and receiving lines and scores of snapshot like glimpses of our life of diplomatic duties and State luxuries.

As my head begin to clear I found myself under the leafed arch of elms, still locked arm in arm with my Ambassador, his big, wide smile now directed purely at me. Was he saying something? I couldn't quite hear. "Pardon," I managed. "Pardon me, I didn't quite hear."

"I asked if you'd prefer to take a handsome cab or walk through the park," he said through that smile.

"The cab," I said through my own growing smile. No wonder I had difficulty hearing him, that smile of his was damn disarming and certain to demand you're full and complete attention.

He was so the gentleman. As the cab pulled up he held the door open with one hand and offered the other to me, as an assist into the carriage. It was a good thing too, for just as I'd mounted the stair and begun my assent into the passenger compartment the horse shook her massive body and shuffled her feet. I assume she was perturbed by our delay and anxious to get moving again and to that she succeeded for the entire carriage violently shook beneath her weight and movements and I all but fell to the pavement. I would have, but the man of my dreams turned out to be as quick and strong and gallant as he was handsome. He caught me in his arms and in the same deft movement mounted the carriage and carried us both to the relatively soft repose of the horsehair covered cushions where he deposited my now trembling body before resting his own at my side.

If the description of our assent into the coach sounds drippy or a bit more suited to the remembrances of a schoolgirl so be it. I've already said the night and my knight were dreamy. It was like living a fairy tale and this time I was Cinderella.

Our ride through the park lasted well into the night. I wouldn't even guess the amount of our bill, people usually hire such rides by the hour or even half-hour yet our ride lasted and lasted and lasted. Finally, when sleep was about to overcome me, he bent to cover my face with his and placed his lips where I knew they belonged. That kiss, our first kiss, was deep and passionate and full of all the things a really good kiss should be. Like the ride, it lasted and lasted and lasted.

Our arrival back at the embassy was an event in and of itself. From a distance on the darkened street the entire building seemed aglow. There were lights burning in every window and several people - departing guests no doubt - milled around on the porch and front steps. Hearing the clip-clop of the horse's hooves as we approached them, they looked up. Our carriage pulled near the curb, the driver jumped down and opening our door he dropped a small-hinged step to assist us disembark. The Ambassador, my Ambassador, exited first. Upon realizing whom it was arriving by carriage, the guests applauded. It wasn't a loud and thunderous applause like you might hear at the end of a play, but rather a quiet and subdued salute to the man of the hour, their returning host. They were acknowledged by a short nod of his head and that smile. Then turning that smile toward me, he extended his hand and brought me out and to his side.

The applause began once more and he tightened his arm around my waist. Looking directly into my eyes he said the words that sealed our fate and confirmed my belief that he was to be and indeed had already become my boyfriend. He smiled that smile once more and said, "We're home, my love, we're home."

My conscious return to the morning shower was not so abrupt this time. It felt like slowly waking up. The memories of our meeting, of the carriage ride and all that took place between us after we'd returned to this house were just that, memories. My shower was complete and I turned off the faucet. Stepping from the shower, water dripping from my naked skin, both my body and my mind were refreshed, my body by the shower and my mind by the knowing - he was mine and he was out there in our bed waiting for me now.

Taking care that my still wet feet didn't slip on the smooth marble tile I crossed the floor to the basin. Again I turned on the hot water, this time preparing to shave. My hand instinctively retrieved a gold handled safety razor from a small alcove to my left. Over the basin the mirror had already begun to fog and I reached up to wipe an oval of the silver surface clean.

The man in the mirror was in his mid-twenties. Mid-length shocks of medium blonde hair still stuck to his forehead, damp and matted from the shower. A modest amount of stubble sprouted from the upper lip and chin. I wiped the mirror again. "Yup. It's me, Chad White." I rubbed my hand across that stubble, feeling the roughness of it on my palm and thought, "I'm pretty ordinary. What ever did he see in me?" Then raising the razor to the bottom of what might have been sideburns if I could grow sideburns, I slowly dragged it down my cheek. Not having bothered with shaving cream or gel or soap, and even though the blade was new, it grabbed at those little hairs, pulling each one and reminding me that I was now fully awake.

As I stared at the reflection of myself in the mirror more of our life together emerged. It was a life of luxury and ease though not lacking in responsibilities. There were social commitments, political and cultural events to attend; the opening of this, the anniversary of that... our calendar was full. Still, he found time for me. Inner disbursed among the required attendance were quiet dinners and walks in the park. We took frequent vacations to exotic locations and also spent time at home.

Home - that's what the embassy had become. Looking deep into the mirror as I finished my shave, I remembered those early nights when our love was new. After the staff had gone home and the house was ours alone, we'd explore. He taught me to appreciate each artifact, each piece of art. We found the wine cellar deep down in the basement. We visited the past in vast trunks of clothing and volumes of scrapbooks of photographs now stored in the attic. Like school kids, we'd chase each other down the long halls, darting in and out of the seemingly endless array of rooms. Our favorite game was hide and seek. One of us would count to one hundred while the other, barefoot so as not to reveal his direction, ran to a hiding place in this mansion of ours. When we found each other that game would switch to tag, one chasing the other until caught we'd collapse into a pile. Sweaty and panting from exhaustion we'd still find the energy to engage another game, a game of love and lust and lasciviousness.

We made love everywhere in that great house. We found each other amid the art and on top of rich oriental carpets. We discovered our depths on the huge oak table dominating the dining room. He took me in the library amid the classics and in the pantry with the pots and pans. We quite literally couldn't get enough of each other and never tired of trying. He was an affectionate lover, tender and warm hearted and attentive to my needs, my desires. He brought me gifts and showered me with his attention. We were happy. We were in love.

I closed my mind with that final thought - love. "It's a good place to stop," I thought; as I dried my face then wet it again with just the right amount of aftershave. The astringent sting consummated my conviction that the man lying in the bed out there was indeed my lover, my soul mate, the object of my deepest desires. Turning, I walked naked, clean and confidently into the bedroom.

My clothing was laid out on a small dressing stand. A crisply starched shirt waited to be paired with freshly pressed slacks. On the floor beneath them my shoes sat perfectly polished. There was a chair and a dressing table. The chair had been pulled invitingly back and the table held a folded copy of the morning newspaper and a steaming cup of freshly brewed coffee. A butler, no doubt the same one who had chosen and laid out my clothing, had also anticipated my intellectual mood. The newspaper was turned to the literary section.

Admittedly the aromatic cup of coffee tempted me but still, I walked past it. I walked past the paper, and past the apparel laid out and pressed. With that one thought, love, still overwhelming my mind and legislating my awareness I crossed the room to his side of our bed. Gently pulling the blankets back, a last thought crept past my consciousness. "To hell with dressing for work." Then I slid my naked body next to his, and kissed him awake.

CHAPTER TWO
Tuesday

"What the fuck!" A buzzing, louder than a fire alarm, blasts me awake.

Eyes open!

My head aches, my body hurts and that damned buzzing still smashes my senses and shatters what remains of my nerves. "What the fuck!"

Twisting my neck the pain increases but at least now I can see what's making the foghorn blast threatening to burst my skull and spill my brains all over the sheets. It's my alarm clock trying to tell me to get my ass up and get ready for work. Lifting my head I strain to see the time.

Six o'clock. Six fucking o'clock! How the fuck can it be six o'clock already? It feels like I just crawled into bed. Oh yeah, I remember, I did just crawl into bed.

Stretching my arm I bend it in a most unnatural and uncomfortable way to reach the obnoxious appliance and slap its disgusting voice silent. How my head aches.

My head drops back on the pillow, take a deep breath and let it out. The death rattle that escapes my lips frightens me and I begin to cough. Next to me my boyfriend stirs. His is in a deeper sleep that even this fit of coughing cannot disturb. I sit up. Throwing my legs over the edge of the bed I feel like throwing my guts up as well. Maybe it's my lack of sleep or that it's just too damn early but I'm confused. This doesn't feel like my body. It doesn't feel like my life. And much to my chagrin, it feels all too familiar. I am going to throw up! On weak legs I stumble from the bed and rush to the bathroom.

Puke. There's a reason they call it puke. It looks like puke. It smells like puke. It tastes like puke. I flush the toilet to hasten its exit from my sight. The water swirls down the drain with a defining noise. It's not as obnoxious as the alarm was, and watching the yellow-brown bile as it spins around the bowl I think to myself that puke isn't so obnoxious either. Hey, I'm feeling better for having released it.

I sit there a minute, my head resting on the cold hard porcelain. I try to decide if the puke is all done. I retch once, maybe twice but nothing comes out. No, I think it's over.

I flush the bowl again. Now it's clean and so are my guts. Still, I don't move. My eyes are closed. As the water rushes back to fill the toilet the air feels cool on my face. It smells fresh and clean, or as fresh and clean as a toilet can smell. I open my eyes and realize that clean is a relative term. The porcelain is yellow and stained. A brown ring circles the bowl just above the water line. The fixture is old and cold and now I realize that the term fresh is just as relative.

The tiles aren't marble. They're dingy and cracked and caked with crud in the corners. Once again that single thought fills my mind, "What the fuck!"

Slowly lifting myself to my feet I wipe the sides of my mouth dry and run my fingers through greasy hair. Something is different. Something is drastically different.

A cracked mirror calls my attention though I hesitate to

look. "Maybe I'd better take in more of my surroundings first," I say to myself.

The room is small, hardly big enough for the toilet, sink and tub. Over in one corner crumpled towels and some dirty underwear lie in a pile. A waste can overflows in the other. Diffused light filters through a dirty shade that is pulled half down to cover an even dirtier window. The walls were probably painted white at one time, though they've long since turned dingy grey. The paint is cracked and patches of plaster have fallen away in places to reveal diagonal stripes of lattice boards.

"What the fuck!"

I gather the courage and drag myself to the mirror. It's as old as the rest of the room, original no doubt. In addition to the crack running corner-to-corner, small patches of silvering have gone missing here and there. It's smeared with something that looks like dried blood. I wipe at the smear and stare. A ghostly pale and overly gaunt man stares back at me. His face is covered with stubble. A crust of something awful dries near the corners of his mouth. His eyes are sunken and sitting on dark pouches of protruding skin. I instantly recognize him, its Chadwick White.

"Hello Chad," I mockingly say out loud. "How's life treating you this morning?"

I don't answer myself. I already know the answer.

On the side of the sink there's a mirror. A single-edged razor blade lies partially covering a raised line of white powder. I lift the blade, careful to grab the proper edge. With the other edge I shape the line and draw it perpendicular toward myself. I contemplate its size, the straightness of its design; I even contemplate how the fine white crystals have been reduced to their now powdery form. Funny, I can't remember that I ever contemplated what that powder might be. I simply dropped my face to an inch from the mirror and with a tremendous snorting sound, sucked it all into my left nostril.

Its effect was immediate. My eyes were wide open and things were crystal clear. My nasal cavities burned like fire. Within seconds I was back on the floor, my head over the bowl, retching the rest of my stomach contents.

"What the fuck!"

I'm not sure how long I hung over the edge of that precipice. It felt like hours though only minutes probably passed. However long, I eventually flushed my guts down the drain and again made the effort to get onto my feet. You'd think after that I'd be wise, but I found myself checking that small silver plate of powdery glass, making sure I'd inhaled everything off its surface. Wouldn't want to waste it after all.

I opened the tap and heard the water splashing into the sink. Back in the mirror I studied the face that I knew was my own. I guess it didn't look that worse for wear. I was sure I could pull it together, make a go of it. Hell, hadn't I looked this way and felt this bad virtually every morning of every day of my entire life?

That thought seemed funny for a moment, though only for a moment. Way back in the deepest depths of my mind I seemed to recall a better time, a time of luxury and ease and unbridled contentment. For that brief time the bathroom was filled with linens and fluffy soft towels. There were sensuous smells coming from soaps and from small bottles containing lotions and au de toilets. Then I snapped back to reality. There was nothing luxurious about this bathroom, and the au de toilet smelled like the toilet and the puke that I'd just flushed away.

"Must be a past life," I mused. "It's certainly not in my present condition."

I felt the water where the tap had been running. It takes a long time for the cold to run hot in these older buildings. I'm going to be late if I wait, I thought, and began splashing less than luke warm water on my face. I pulled on the mirror that opened in my hands. From the cabinet behind I extracted the familiar red can of shaving cream. I filled my hand with a generous dollop of foam which, using my other hand, I immediately began transferring to my chin.

"Can't be late again Chad," I said to the mirror. "You'll lose this shitty job like all the others."

I reached back to the cabinet and fumbled for a disposable razor. I hate using old ones, but the package was empty leaving me with no choice. I considered checking to try and figure out which one had the least amount of miles on its blade but again sensing the need for speed I gave up and took the closest. "Hurry your little ass, Mr. White."

I should have waited for the hot water, I thought as the cold sliver of steel began ripping the short hairs from my chin. I winced and jerked my head back. I should have remembered to buy new blades. But I didn't, I thought as I continued to assault my face.

Stopping only to rinse stubble flecked foam from the razor; I pulled long swatches of beard away from my skin. The pain of pulling those hairs began to actually feel good. Each pinch provided another opportunity to wake up, to focus.

I wasn't focused enough. A sudden pain shot through me and a red bead of liquid leaked out from under the blade.

"Shit," I yelled. Instinctively I dropped the razor and slapped at the blood. Something or someone in the room beyond made a sound. I twisted my body and, with my other hand, snatched a sheet of toilet paper from the roll hanging off the wall by the toilet. I tore a corner of tissue and applied it to my face. The porous white paper quickly turned red and stuck to my skin. Reaching back for the razor I bumped the mirror from which, moments earlier, I'd cut the line. It teetered on the edge of the sink and I unsuccessfully made an effort to stabilize but it fell, smashing to bits on the floor.

"What the fuck!" This time the words weren't just in my mind. They'd come from the bedroom. The breaking glass had shaken my boyfriend from sleep. Looking over my shoulder I could see him stirring.

"Sorry."

"Sorry my ass," came his reply. "What the fuck are you doing in there?"

"I'm getting myself ready to go to work," I yelled back. "You should be doing the same."

"Fuck," was his only response.

My boyfriend, I thought, now there's a prize. I retrieved the razor and resumed the assault, but my mind stayed on the stranger in the other room. How much did I really know about him?

Lets see... he was lazy, a drunk. He did drugs, lots of drugs. He was sarcastic and sometimes caustic, and oh yea, he was a hell of a great fuck.

I remember the first night we met. I'd gone to the club with a few of my friends. The night had been hot and the D.J. hotter. We'd been on the dance floor for hours, leaving only to make our way to the bar and an unceasing supply of shots. Sweat was streaming from my skin and, like almost everyone else, my shirt had long since become history. My mind was filled with lights and music and the half-naked bodies that writhed all around. It was one of those magical nights when lust and maybe even love was in the air.

My bladder was bursting so I excused myself and pushed through the mob making my way to the back of the room where, as expected, I found a line of people waiting for a stall and relief. Though I took up a place at the back of the line more people kept coming and soon there were as many people waiting behind me as in front.

"This is amazing," said a voice from behind. "One second you're at the end of the line and the next second you're in the middle."

"What's so amazing about that," I said turning to see if it was anyone I knew. "The bar's crowded and people gotta pee."

He was young, at least younger than I was. Like me, his shirt was off and his body covered in sweat. It was thin and tight and I liked the way the sweat glistened on his flat stomach muscles.

"I was just thinking," he said through a smile. "If you can get to the middle of the line this fast why does it take forever to reach the front?"

I laughed, which was exactly what he had wanted me to do. The ice having been broken he continued in conversation. It was just the usual stuff. He told me his name -- which was Robbie -- and asked for mine. He wanted to know if I came here often - I did. He asked who I knew - almost everyone. He was interested in whether I liked the music - yes, a lot. And, he wondered if I'd been here for the last great party - nope, missed it. Before long we found ourselves at the front of the line and in front of the washroom. The door opened and the previous party popped out. "Who's next," he said, holding the door open.

"We are," replied Robbie. He grabbed my arm and, pulling a very startled me into the men's room, closed the door and locked it.

"Ah, what's going on? I asked.

"This!" He exclaimed, as he pulled my body into his and pressed his lips to mine.

An even more startled me pried him away and reached for the door.

"Not so fast, hot stuff. Now that you've tasted my lips, taste this." He reached into the pocket of his tight blue jeans and extracted a small white paper package. With a flick of his fingers the package was open revealing the treasure within. His other hand produced a short piece of drinking straw. In one movement he raised one end of the straw to my nostril and inserted the other end into the powder.

"You do candy, don't you?"

Still startled, I shook my head yes and tried to say sure. He jerked his hands back.

"Careful, baby! Don't want to spill any of this stuff. It's quality."

Carefully, he brought his hands back to my nose. This time I didn't say a word but allowed him to insert his straw into my nostril.

"Ok baby, the first half's yours," he said locking his eyes on mine.

I held his gaze and inhaled with a quick snort. The effect was immediate. First it burned. I could feel it singe every hair in my nostril. In a nanosecond the burning was replaced by cold. It traveled deep into the inner recesses of my nasal cavities and made my face numb. I knew it wasn't coke.

My eyes were still locked on his. I don't know why but I couldn't look away. They were deep, and blue, really blue. There was a liquid quality to them. They seemed to grow bigger. Or was it my eyes just dilating? I didn't know. I didn't care. I just wanted to fall deeper into the blueness that they held.

I'm not sure how long we stared into each other's souls but I'm sure that's what I was doing, just as I know with out a doubt that he was doing the same. From that instant, we were inextricably linked. A smile crossed his lips. At least I think it did. I wasn't looking at his lips, only his eyes, and they were smiling. He moved the straw from my nose to his and repeated my action, then crumpled the now empty packet and dropped it to the floor.

This time I was the one who reached out to him. I pulled his body close to mine and wrapped my arms around it.

I could feel the dampness of his sweat soaked shirtless skin pressing tightly to my own. Our eyes didn't blink. As the drug took hold, I felt our fluids intermingle. His body felt thinner and tighter than it had looked. I could feel his breathing, the beating of his heart, and the beating of my own. Looking deeper into those eyes I felt our heartbeats start to synchronize and as they did I let myself go. I fell, body and soul, into him. I was lost.

We held each other for a long time, neither saying a word. Our lips again found each other, our tongues intertwined. More of our fluids combined. I wanted him, wanted all of him. I wanted to literally be inside of him. I wanted to experience every aspect of him. I wanted to be him.

We were in that men's room a long time. We could have stayed even longer but insistent knocking from the other side of the door broke our concentration as well as our embrace. I remembered the line of other guys waiting to pee and reluctantly released Robbie from my arms. They fell to my side.

"Damn," I stammered. "I'm pretty fucked up. Maybe I should go home."

"Maybe we should go to the dance floor," was Robbie's reply.

Somehow we both stumbled back into the club. We were pretty fucked up, but we'd found each other and basically never let each other go. The drugs and Robbie and now the music all vied for position inside me. I alternated between them, letting each take a turn in a seemingly endless assault on my senses. Eventually I grew used to the effect of the drugs and my high leveled. The music let go when they announced, "Last call". But Robbie's grip on me never diminished. It was lust, if not love, at first sight.

The powder Robbie pushed up my nose in the men's room turned out to be meth so sleep eluded us that night and for most of the next day. I think we crashed sometime the next evening but even that seems a bit foggy. All I remember with any clarity is that I succeeded in my desire to be inside him. I entered that boy's butt again and again and after we rested I re-entered him. I never came. The drugs wouldn't let me, but I didn't care. I was hard. He was hard. The sex went on for hours stopping only occasionally when Robbie produced a small brown bottle and we took another snort. The drug of choice this time was cocaine. "A meth buzz lasts too long. Coke mellows you out," Robbie had explained. "It takes the edge off." Much later we both popped a lude, or at least what he called a lude, and sleep overwhelmed our high.

I didn't really wake up as much as I simply opened my eyes in a return to consciousness. I found myself half smeared with shave cream, a small piece of blood soaked tissue sticking to my chin, looking a bit worse for wear before that cracked mirror. It took a few seconds for my mind to catch up but I soon remembered. "Ah yes, Chad White, you're getting ready to go to work." Turning my head I called out, "Hey Robbie, what time is it?"

There was no reply from the bedroom, just silence. Clearly, Robbie had fallen back to sleep. I called again, "Robbie!"

Nothing.

Cupping my hands, I captured some tap water and splashed the shaving cream from my face. The water was still cold. Looking up at my reflection I noticed the tissue still stuck to my skin, though it was now soaked and more matted. I turned and walked back in the bedroom. The alarm clock sat on the seat of a straight-backed wooden chair pulled next to my side of the bed. The chair served as my nightstand and the clock as my torturer, ripping me from sleep, replacing the last night's buzz with its own. Robbie bought me that clock so I wouldn't be late for work. Drugs - acquiring them, packaging them, selling and using them - that was Robbie's job so he didn't really work. As a consequence, he didn't really get out of bed until the mood struck him. Usually that mood came about noon, sometimes as late as two or three. This morning, as I bent over to check the time on my clock, it was evident that the mood would strike later, not sooner.

He laid there, covers kicked off and naked as the day he was born. The rhythm of his breathing pushed his chest up and down, but that tight, flat stomach of his never moved. Lowering my gaze I took in the little patch of precisely trimmed hair that trimmed a perfect cock draped over perfect balls. At least they were perfect for me. And I knew without seeing it that if I turned him over I'd find an equally perfect butt -- smooth and round and firm and all mine. At least I was pretty sure it was all mine. I used it enough, but who knows, maybe he was selling that in addition to the drugs.

Drugs. Drugs, drugs, drugs… just thinking about them had wet my appetite for another bump. Robbie's jeans were laying there in a heap next to the bed. I bent down to pick them up. As I did, I brought my face to within inches of his. I was so close that if I inhaled as he exhaled, our breath would be one. I moved my head and brushed my lips over his, past his chin and across the smoothness of his chest. Dragging them down the flat, hairless belly I stopped short of the prize. Sorry baby, I thought, this morning I choose door number two. Reaching my hand into the pocket of his crumpled jeans, I felt for the bottle I knew would be there.

Back in the bathroom I twisted the cap off the bottle intending to shake a pile of its contents onto the mirror that I expected to find sitting on the sink. It wasn't there. "Fuck me with a rock." The words escaped my mouth before I'd let the coke escape the bottle. "Now where the fuck did the mirror go?" I know you won't believe me but to tell you the truth, I'd forgotten that I'd smashed it on the floor just moments ago. And, when I found it, in pieces piled into the corner, half hidden by a dirty towel, it surprised me. "What the fuck happened here?"

That's the way it is when you're using. Everyday life eludes you. You do things you can't remember doing and forget to do things you're supposed to remember to do.

Oh well, I thought as I tapped the bottle on the sink letting it deposit a small pile on the porcelain. Faster than you could say fuck, it was up my nose and out of sight. I considered tapping it again but I knew Robbie would know some was missing. I didn't need to argue with him. Instead, I replaced the cap - twisting it tightly so it couldn't spill - and placed it on the sink where the pile had just been. Must remember to put it back in his pocket, I thought just before that last snort invaded my mind and wiped such concerns away.

My nostrils burned like I'd inhaled hot coals from an old fire. I squeezed my eyes closed tight. I was familiar with this burning and relished the way it took hold of my being. Eyes still closed, I sucked a quick blast of air up my nose and with it, the last vestiges of powder still clinging to the short hairs on the insides of my nose. Damn, I enjoyed this burn. Reaching out I fumbled for the faucet, twisted it sharply to the right then dropped my hand to the water it produced. Raising that hand to my face I inserted a finger into each side of that burning nose and inhaled again. This time a cold moistness quenched the fire and dampened the dried out lining of my nasal cavities.

The water felt internally refreshing. I opened my eyes and looked around.

At first I can't figure out where the fuck I am. It's a restaurant for sure, but what restaurant and how did I get here.

"Will someone be joining you?"

I spin around. A waiter looks quizzically at me but I don't reply.

"Sir? Just one?"

"Huh," I'm still trying to make sense of this shift in consciousness.

"I'm asking if anyone will be joining you or not. After that I'm going to ask if you prefer smoking or non-smoking, so you might want to start mulling that over." The waiter smiled. His small attempt at humor didn't sit well with me and I wanted to reply with some caustic remark but my mind was still fogged and I couldn't think of one fast enough. Fuck it, I though and was just about to tell him I'd dine alone when a hand squeezed my shoulder.

"He's joining me."

I looked around. "Oh, thank God," I said, "Finally a face I recognize."

Robbie let his hand slip off my shoulder and down to my waist. Pulling me toward him, he guided me to an empty table in the otherwise crowded room. He literally pushed me down into a chair. As I plopped my butt down his leg went up. Swinging it up over my knees and facing me, he slapped his own butt down on my lap.

"Thank God you're here," he gushed, "I thought I'd have to find someone else to fuck tonight."

I opened my mouth to protest that I wasn't really comfortable with him on my lap when he shouted; "Kiss me you fool!" then shoved his tongue between my lips and down my throat.

Mortified. I was mortified now and whenever he did things like this in public places but what could I do? He thought it was fun and he damn sure wasn't going to stop. What could I expect; he all but assaulted me in that men's room on the night we met. Robbie was impulsive and sexual and oh so fucking cute. I gave in to his boy games and kissed him back. Across the room I noticed the waiter was glaring at us in one of those "why don't you two get a room" kind of ways. I didn't care. Hell, everyone in the dining room was staring at us. Some had the waiter's thoughts in their eyes but there were plenty of others who looked jealous or envious or like they just wished to fuck some cute kid would grind his ass into them for a change.

My "kid's" cute ass extracted itself from my lap. Robbie reached out and took my arm. In a voice way too loud for just talking to me he said, "Come on, let's go to the bathroom and wash our hands." Then he led me the long way around the room to a set of matching doors and the facilities beyond.

Needless to say, we didn't wash our hands in the men's room - didn't even pee though our pants were down. I had him up on the sink, his cute bubble butt filling the basin and his smooth hairless legs up in the air. Most people can only think of one thing to do with a sink in a bathroom but we knew there were three. To be sure you could wash your hands, but you could also fuck in them and do drugs on them. That night we did two of those three things before returning to our table and placing our orders with the disapproving waiter.

That was the way my life with Robbie was - Sex, Drugs and Rock-n-Roll, except the "rock" was usually crack or cocaine and the "roll" was a roll in the hay.

Robbie's "job" kept him up most nights; mine got me up most mornings. It was a difficult schedule that only worked with drugs. We used them to get up and again to go to sleep. Hell, we used them all the times, if the truth be told. We'd talked about him stopping selling. It was a big risk. But our personal addictions were totally tied to his job's benefits - we didn't pay to play. As another benefit, we were among the most popular people in the party pool. Our cell phones - well, his mostly - never quit ringing. There were always people pressing us to come out, to meet them in the clubs.

Being popular has its advantages but they come at a cost. I can't tell you the number of times I've gone home alone. There were club dates and after parties and after-after parties. Robbie was expected to attend them all. Me? As I told you, I was still holding down a regular job. As difficult as it was, I was the one who would drag his worn out body home and throw myself into an empty bed night after night while Robbie went on. With few exceptions he did come home, but he'd come home at 4 or 5 o'clock in the morning while I'd come home at midnight.

Robbie always woke me up when he came to bed. In the hazy fog of a half-slept night, we'd rip one off; I'd drop an Ambien and again find sleep.

Last night had been one of those nights and this morning, while Robbie still slept, I was struggling to dress for work. Like most mornings, it was hell. If only I had another bump.

Just to get me going, I thought, trying to figure out how much I'd already done since leaving him lying in bed. I looked back at him there now. He was snoring. I wanted to wake him, to make him get up and fix me something to eat. Damn, if I have to get out of bed why shouldn't he? I was going to shake his ass up, but I knew that if I did I still wouldn't get bacon and eggs. He was just too damn cute and I knew the mere sight of him would invoke my other desires. Food usually took a back seat to sex and always to drugs.

It wasn't the cocaine. I know some people can't eat on coke and there are a lot of people who go soft on the stuff, making a fuck all but impossible. But, neither Robbie nor I shared that affliction. Coke made me horny and, like smoking weed, we'd both get the munchies. Robbie was always horny. You'd swear he was a woman given his propensity for multiple orgasms. It was crystal that kept us skinny -- Methamphetamine, the gay equivalent to the South Beach Diet. A steady supply of our girlfriend, Tina, also helped diffuse the conflicts in our sleeping schedules. When we were tweaking we just didn't sleep. Oh, we still went to bed, but for other purposes. And, we didn't really need the bed. Robbie and I fucked wherever and whenever we felt the urge. You see Tina also erased what little inhibitions we had. As I thought about all the places where we'd done it, the sink at that restaurant seemed relatively tame.

I finished up in the bathroom, turned off the faucet and made my way back to the bedroom. It was a mess. There were piles of dirty laundry sitting on top of piles of dirty laundry. The remnants from weeks of take-out littered the spaces in between those piles. Dresser drawers stood open and I rummaged through them. Half of what I found there looked dirty and nothing seemed to match. Damn, I thought, I need a shirt.

Looking around, I searched the room for something to

wear. It needed to be relatively clean and somewhat wrinkle free. I picked up a few things but put them back down. I found one shirt hanging from the back of a chair that didn't seem too bad. At least it had been hanging so there weren't many wrinkles. But it proved unworthy. One of us had worn it to the clubs and it reeked of stale cigarettes and even more stale beer. Keep looking. For a moment I considered a blue button-down which was crunched up under one of the empty pizza boxes. I could wear it under a sweater. But I discarded it when I realized I'd never find a sweater.

As I searched the room I eventually rediscovered that small pile lying on the floor near the bed, next to Robbie. I'll bet his shirt is clean, I considered as I bent over to reach for it. But my hand never touched his shirt. It never made it past his pants. Instinctively, I was back in his pockets feeling around for the bottle. Where the fuck did it go?

I probably only searched for a moment or so, but when you're high things seem to take forever. It felt like my hands were in those pants for hours. Finally it struck me. The bottle, the cocaine, Robbie's stash was still sitting on the bathroom sink - the last place I'd used it. It might have seemed like I was fumbling around in his pockets for ever but it was only a flash before I found myself back in the bathroom, head bowed low over the sink.

You probably think I've exceeded my limit. Was it four? Did I do three bumps this morning? Maybe I did five. The truth is I never counted, and I don't just mean this morning. I never, ever keep track of my drugs. If I did I'd probably go twelve-step or something. No. I never keep track but that doesn't mean I don't have my limits and this morning I was fairly certain that I hadn't exceeded them. All I had to do was find a shirt, put it on and make my way to the bus stop and work. All I had to do was find a shirt.

I picked the little brown bottle up off of the sink and poured the remainder of its contents out in a pile on the porcelain. Bending over, I took it all in a single snort. I closed my eyes but I didn't straighten up. I savored the sensation. I'd done enough that it no longer burned, but a slow numb was reaching my brain. I opened my eyes and my prayers were answered. There on the floor, in the corner under the sink, amid the shards of broken glass, under the towel - there it was. My shirt!

I think I put it on, but maybe not. It's possible that I put it on then took it back off. All I know is I found myself back in the bedroom, still half naked and still no where near ready to go to work. Robbie was still sleeping and I cursed him for that ability. Why was it that I had to be up? Why was it that I had to get dressed? And, why was it that no one ever did laundry around this place?

"Fuck you!" I yelled. "Fuck you, bastard. Get the fuck out of bed"

Robbie rolled over and forced his eyes open. They locked on mine.

"Hey, what's up?"

"I'm looking for a shirt to wear and you're not helping," I told him, trying to sound angry.

Robbie reached out and threw the covers back. My eyes left his and traveled down the length of body. His small frame was naked, and smooth, and very inviting.

"Come under here and see if you can find a shirt," he said smiling. "And lose that fucked up attitude, Mary."

I thought about it for a second or so. What the fuck. I had sick days coming, work wasn't all that important.

CHAPTER THREE
Wednesday

Isn't it funny how you sometimes wake up before the alarm goes off? It's like you've got an internal alarm clock that somehow knows to wake you just moments before the real alarm clock is set to go off. This morning, my internal alarm clock opened my eyes and told me to get out of bed. I didn't. Not at first anyway. I just lay there staring at the ceiling. I was trying to remember exactly where I was. In the back of my mind I knew it was my bedroom but… well, you know the story.

Lying next to me I could feel the warmth of his body deep in an undisturbed slumber. His own internal alarm wasn't working like mine, or if it was it was set to some other time. Glancing to my left, my eyes searched for the red glowing digits on the clock radio that I knew would sit on the nightstand next to my bed. Five fifty-nine. Damn, my internal clock was precise.

Under the covers I could still feel the man whose body touched mine and I wondered what he looked like. I could find out if I just lifted those covers. I didn't lift them, not yet. I just lay there staring at the digital glow, waiting six o'clock and the audible confirmation that my internal clock kept perfect time. Shortly thereafter my expectations were met. The last digit, nine, transformed itself into a zero and virtually simultaneously the one next to it morphed a five into a second zero. Inevitably, the first digit, the one on the left of those two blinking dots, jumped from five to six and the buzzer went off.

I stared. I should have shut it off right away. If I'd been more considerate, I would have shut it off even before it announced the allotted time for me to wake-up. I knew the buzzing might wake my boyfriend, but I didn't care. For once, I thought, he can get up first and see who's lying in bed next to him.

I continued to stare at the clock until the last zero on the right hand side had become a one, then slowly slid my hand from beneath the sheets and pressed the little black button to silence the noise. I rolled to the right.

Sliding my other hand toward him I let my fingers feel his flesh. Softly and slowly they slid down his side. He didn't stir. My hand traveled south tracing the treasure trail of short hairs running from his navel to his cock. Just before reaching that prize, the hairs exploded into a tangle of wiry curls. I let my fingers lose themselves there, twisting and turning the curls, resisting the temptation to touch his tool.

I never did grope him, not that I didn't want to. Instead, I moved my hand back up his stomach, across his chest and to a point just under his chin. Then, with a slow motion movement I gently pulled the covers away from his face. After having let the alarm blast as long as it did I'm not sure why I was being so careful not to wake him now. I guess it was just my curiosity. Since he didn't wake up when I wanted him to, I thought I'd use the opportunity to see if I could figure out his story - our story - before he did open his eyes.

The man in bed with me was old. I was shocked at how old he was. There were age lines in the rough skin of his face, particularly around his eyes and near the corners of his lips. I can't say he was wrinkled. But his face revealed the fact that he had enough years under his belt to have been my father. His hair was thinning. It was grey near the temples.

Letting my head roll back, my eyes again found the ceiling, which I stared at until its white emptiness enveloped my mind and cleared it of thoughts. I continued to lie there, flat on my back, until a single thought returned. It was the one thought which would motivate my migration from the security of the bed sheets to the bathroom beyond. Staring at the empty white space above my head, it came - if he's that old, I thought, how the fuck old am I?

I don't really know why but that thought scared the heck out of me. It shouldn't have. I mean it's not like everyone doesn't grow old. And your life doesn't end 'cause your hair recedes. Still, I needed to make it to the mirror and find out if my hair was receding. I needed to know if my skin was sagging. The skin on the man lying next to me certainly was, and I needed to know if that man - my man - was my age. Worse than that I needed to assure myself that, between me and my boyfriend, he wasn't the youngster!

I was moving so fast I didn't bother to take in the furnishings. I didn't observe the art or how clean the room was or wasn't. This morning the bathroom was situated at the end of a hall, and reaching it, I couldn't even tell you how many other rooms I'd passed. In short, I had none of my usual clues from which to deduce the situation. This morning, the knowledge of my boyfriend's identity and our life together would take a back seat to the ever more pressing problem. If he was that old, how the fuck old was I?

The bathroom was dark. There was a window but the Sun hadn't risen and the shades were still drawn. Instinctively, I knew where the light switch would be. My fingers flicked at the switch but it didn't come on. Instead, I could hear the soft whine of an exhaust fan as it sucked at the stillness but illuminated nothing. My fingers felt left and right until I found another switch and pushed it up. Momentarily blinded by the blast of incandescence that followed, I rubbed my eyes and waited for them to focus. When they did I was shocked. There in the mirror was me, Chadwick White. I was a young Chadwick White, a very young Chadwick White.

I blinked then blinked again. Maybe I'm dreaming, still sleeping. Perhaps the desire not to be old was being compensated by a less than truthful reflection. I rubbed my eyes and looked again. Nope. I was still young. I was still very young.

I'm not all that good at guessing an age. I knew that the man back in bed was at least fifty, but that being said, he could have been sixty or even a bit older. I, on the other hand, looked to be in my late teens. I ran my hand through thick shocks of blond hair, pulling it back from my forehead. It was anything but receding. There was a trace of acne on my otherwise smooth skin and my cheeks boasted baby fat and a rosy red blush. Damn, I'm eighteen or nineteen if I'm a day, I thought. And, that geezer back in the bed is a child molester.

I was still somewhat in a state of shock as I slipped my shorts off and stepped into the shower. I didn't wait for the water to warm, didn't test it before I turned the knob. I didn't care. I just wanted to soap my skin and wash myself clean. I'd just gotten out of bed with a man twice or three times my age and I felt dirty and disgusting and - my mind searched for the right adjective. Cheap! That was the word. I felt dirty and disgusting and cheap.

The shower spat its contents with a cleansing blast on my body. I snatched the soap from its tray and began briskly rubbing it all over myself. Soon, mounds of soft suds were smothering my skin. I slid them around with the palms of my hands, feeling my body. It was soft and smooth. With the exception of my own mound of pubic hair, it felt like a baby's bottom. Devoid of even the hint of stubble, I wondered if I were even old enough to shave. I rubbed the soap harder, hoping to remove the realization that the body of the man I was sleeping with was anything but soft and smooth and supple.

I had an erection. Without ever having touched my dick, it was standing at attention hard as a rock. I guessed that was more evidence of my age. No need for Viagra, I thought. Morning wood is Mother Nature's reward to youth.

"Oh well," I said right out loud. "Never look a gift horse in the mouth." Wrapping my soap slippery hand around that erection, I proceeded to rub one out.

I lost myself in self-satisfaction, letting my body be my lover if only for this moment. After a few moments my efforts paid off. I was gripped by a series of rapid convulsions. My muscles stiffened and my mind went blank. A familiar warm sensation came over me and, arching my back, I let go with my eruption. The effect was immediate just as it was immediately over. My eyes, which had been clenched tightly, closed now fluttered open. My cock dropped from the cradle of my palm and I looked around. I was still in the shower, smooth, soapy and spent.

I half expected to have had a glimpse of my boyfriend in my mind. The act of ejaculation should have triggered some sort of self-realization. But it didn't. Not this time. I was as alone in my mind as I had been alone in my masturbation. I had exhausted myself mentally as well as physically, I thought. I tried to remember what tricks I might use, what triggers might help unlock my memories and begin the process of remember-ing. Who was that guy back in the bedroom? What was our life like together?

Nothing!

I let the shower remove the soap from my skin, and with it, any jizz that still dripped from my dick. A pile of it remained on the floor of the shower. I moved my foot around, smearing it up and allowing it to mix with the water. Soon it had swirled down the drain and a little bit of me was gone forever. In my mind, I searched the rest of me for a clue to who I might be, who he might be and what our life together was like.

Again, nothing!

This is damn strange, I thought. It's like I've got amnesia or something. Clearly I'd recognized myself in the mirror's reflection. I knew my name. I knew my age, or at least that I was young. And, I knew that my boyfriend was a geezer, if he was my boyfriend. I'm thinking if I can't make my mind recall anything about him perhaps there aren't a lot of memories floating around in there. Maybe I don't really know him. Maybe we haven't really spent much time together. Without any impression whatsoever, maybe he's a stranger.

Stranger Danger! I tried that one on for size. What if he's a trick, someone I just picked up on the streets? What if I can't remember him because I've never really known him? What if he's Gacy or Eyler or one of the scores of other infamous creeps who pick up young men, sex and drug them and dismember their tender flesh for fun?

I tripped on that thought for a few seconds but discarded it with the realization that I didn't feel drugged. I wasn't woozy or wobbly on my feet and my mind was clear. In fact, that was the problem. My mind was too clear. I had nothing to go on. It was devoid of clues.

Clues! That's what I need.

I now remembered that I'd been in such a rush to reach the mirror and discover my age that I hadn't bothered to check out the room, or its furnishings, or anything that might have offered a hint of our history. The who, what, where and when of our life together were questions, just questions. I needed some answers and to find answers I needed clues.

I stepped out of my shower and grabbed a towel. Don't miss anything, I admonished myself. Examine your surroundings and sort this all out. Now, what do I see?

The towel in my hand was nondescript, white, medium weight terry-cloth. There were no monograms, no stains. It had been hanging from the wall on a bar of stainless steel. The wall was painted white. I spun around. Everything was white. The sink, the stool, the box of tissues on the back of the stool, were all white. Even the damn soap was white. I was in a cloud, my mind in a fog. Was there anything in this room that wasn't white?

I thought about that question a while then started to laugh. The first answer that had come to mind was me. I'm not white. But that wasn't true. I was white. I was a white man - well, boy - a Caucasian. And I was white in another way too. My name was White, Chad White.

Shit, this is going to be more difficult that I'd thought.

What else is here? The toilet seat is white. The water in the toilet is clear, which might just as well be white. I could take a brown dump in it but what would that prove? It would only be a part of me and I'd already decided that I was White. Keep thinking!

I could have just gone back to the bedroom. I could have woke his old ass up and asked him who the fuck he was and what was he doing with me. I didn't. Instead, I let my thoughts run circles around this white thing. I couldn't get it out of my mind. It was like I was obsessed or something. Perhaps I'd been drugged after all, I recall thinking. It's like I'm dizzy, if not drugged.

Dizzy? Maybe I'm blonde!

I spun back to myself in the mirror. Well, what do you know? I am a blonde, I discovered, trying to remember if I remembered that from the first time I'd searched the mirror and found out I was young. That's when it hit me.

The mirror!

Yea, I know what you're going to say. The mirror is silver which is sort of like clear and, just like the toilet bowl water I've already decided that clear might just as well be white. But that's not what I was thinking at that point in time. I was thinking that there must be something behind that mirror. There must be a medicine cabinet full of stuff. Like a guest at a party, I opened that cabinet to see what my host was hiding.

Pay dirt!

There was stuff alright, lots of it. The cabinet was chock full of crap, lots and lots of very colorful crap. And amid this colorful crap were clues.

The first thing I picked up was most definitely a clue, though it didn't get me any further in my search for answers. Geratol, the elixir of the aged - hell, I already knew he was old. And there was more where that came from. I found a bottle of Metamucil, the mucus mover my grandpa used to mix every morning. There was a roll of wig tape - great, he was bald! And there was a clue that brought me to tears with laughter. I found a package of poly-grip. Yes! He gives good blowjobs!

There were bottles of medicine I knew nothing about, some cleaning products to help keep things white and a few other toiletries but nothing to jog my memory or make me remember who the fuck he was and why I was with him. Better retrace my steps, I thought. The bedroom always has tales to tell.

I was out the door and half down the hall when I stopped. He might be awake. Better not present too pleasing a picture when I walk into the room. He might not be ready to resist my boy perfect presentation. Returning to the bathroom I lifted that bleach white terry-cloth towel off the floor and wrapped it around my waist.

As it turned out, my modesty was unnecessary. The old geezer was still snoring. I set out to search his space. There were cufflinks and several bottles of cologne setting out on the dresser. I opened a few of the bottles and sniffed the cologne but my olfactory detective work was for naught. All I found out was that I favored one of the scents. There were a few I could have taken back to the bath and poured down the drain, but nothing told me anything I needed to know. I picked up the cufflinks and examined them. I turned them over and over in my hand but again, not much there. They were nice and all, pretty as well as pretty nondescript. If I was a hustler, if he were a trick, I could have slipped them into my pocket. I didn't. For one thing, I didn't know if I was a hustler. For another, I was wrapped in a towel. I didn't have any pockets.

The dresser, like the cufflinks, was nondescript. It looked like the stuff you could buy from almost any department store or furnishing outlet in Every Town, USA. I pulled open a drawer. There were neat little rows of rolled up socks. One row was white (surprise, surprise) but another was dark and there was a third row with mixed pairs that appeared to be dress socks. They were thinner and some had designs embroidered on their sides. Not much to go on here, I said to myself as I silently slid the drawer back in place. No sense making noise and waking him up. Like Mattlock or Mulder or Columbo, or any great detective, I continued to collect clues.

There was definitely color in the next drawer I opened. It was filled with a rainbow stack of polo shirts, each ironed and pressed and placed in perfect position so you could pick out just the color you wanted. I deduced the old guy was anal; he maybe even had one of those obsessive-compulsive disorder things. These thoughts were confirmed by the contents of each drawer I slid open. Everything was perfect. It was all pressed and placed in picture perfect position to make it easy to find what you were looking for - except not for me. I was looking for answers and finding only frustration.

At one end of the room was a shelf of books. Here and there trophies and small figurines sat in spaces not occupied by books. I crossed the room and examined the books. I found a few novels, mostly mystery and a few science fictions. The vast majority of volumes were reference works, dictionaries, thesaurus, and a full set of the Encyclopedia Britannica. I wondered if the old guy had heard of the Internet. This little library represented the old way to knowledge. These days you Googled your query and only printed the answers you needed. Right now, I needed some answers that a slew of search engines wouldn't provide.

The trophies gave me my first hint at who he was and what was going on. I guess I was expecting bowling or golf awards given his age, instead I discovered that each trophy had been presented for academic achievement. Well at least that explains the encyclopedias, I thought.

Most of the trophies were inscribed with the name of the competition for which it was the prize. One said Academic Bowl, another bore Knowledge Decathlon. Universities, colleges and other institutions of higher learning had presented some. There were a lot of them, and they all had been awarded for the same rank, First Place.

Ok, I considered, what does this say? He's smart. He's educated. Perhaps he's a college professor or a doctor or something. Clearly, the man I found myself sleeping with was not a blue-collar worker though I couldn't have known that by the clothing I found laying about the room. There wasn't any. I examined it all and every inch of this place was orderly and tidy, neat and clean. In addition to the bookcase and bed there was that big dresser, two night-stands and little else in the nature of furniture. The pieces that were present were nice, but hardly expensive. They were the kind of things you could buy in any of a million furniture stores. What they were though was highly polished.

Opposite the door to the hall that led to the bathroom was another door. Though closed, I figured it must be a closet. The man had to wear clothes and the clothes had to hang somewhere. Moving across to the door I grasped its knob and twisted. Let's see some of your secrets; I said swinging the door open.

I can't say I was surprised by the contents of the smallish room. It contained clothes. Now, if it had been filled with sado-masochistic paraphernalia like whips and chains and black leather suits and stuff, well then I might have been shocked. I might also have gotten a few more clues in my hunt for who he was. Instead I found more of the same. The clothes were all neat and tidy. Everything ironed and hanging in a well thought out order. Shirts to the left, trousers to the right, and four or five pairs of perfectly polished shoes lined up on the floor. Inside each shoe was one of those old-fashioned shoetrees, the things that help hold the shape and keep the shoes looking new. I reminded myself that a good detective doesn't just scratch the surface so I began to examine the clothes more closely, feeling the quality of the material, looking at the cut and reading the labels.

Grandpa has style, I observed. His wardrobe consisted of quality goods of the most popular styles. They all boasted brand names, if not designer labels. He had a great sense of color, a fact most easily observed as everything had been arraigned with the same attention to order as I encountered in the drawer filled with Polo shirts. His dress shirts lacked a little excitement. Like the bathroom, they were all white. Still, they sported quality labels and had been crisply starched and pressed before being hung on their hangers. Oh yeah, he didn't use wire. He had invested in plastic hangers, all matching blue. A few of the hangers that weren't made of plastic were padded. From these he'd hung his more delicate duds. And his suits hung from wood, with bunches of tissue paper placed into each arm to prevent any opportunity for the hanger to disfigure the material. A large collection of silk ties hung from a rack on the wall. They were quality if not overly expensive, and hinted at the same conservatism as the white dress shirts. There weren't any dirty clothes, at least none I could find. Everything in his closet was like everything in his room, picture perfect.

Clearly one of those obsessive-compulsive personalities, I concluded.

Just as I was about to come out of the closet (no pun intended) I spied a black leather attaché on the floor in the corner. Crouching down, I clicked it opened to display its contents. I found it filled with files. Eureka! If this find didn't shed some light on the guy I didn't know what would.

I flipped through each folder, carefully considering their contents. The guy did a lot of research. The files were filled with photocopies, pages from books. There were newspaper clippings and printouts from web sources. Notations in perfect penmanship had been jotted in the margins. Pads of yellow lined paper were filled with copious notes written by the same hand. He was researching something. Scratch that, he was researching lots of things. There were files on various people, places and things. He had a ream of material about a proposed piece of legislation. It had something to do with land laws and how they affected the local school district. There was a folder filled with facts about a new treatment for cancer, and a file with research on the latest, greatest invention for fuel efficiency. I found a few papers pertaining to the death penalty debate, and more about prisons and punishment options for prisoners. I saw a few files on animal rights, and one that compared and contrasted opposing views in the gay marriage debate.

Carefully closing the case, I took pains to place it back in the corner in exactly the same position as I'd found it. Then I sat back on the floor and considered the clues I'd gleaned.

The old guy, my boyfriend I presumed, was intelligent. He did a lot of reading and obviously knew his way around a research library. He was some sort of professional, at least it seemed so from the suits and shirts and ties. And there was the attaché, if that didn't say professional I don't know what did. Its contents? I wondered what they could tell me. Let's see, he did research, that much was clear. He could be a politician, or an attorney. What else could I tell from the things I'd observed?

Though I sat on that floor for what seemed like a lifetime, I eventually came to no conclusions. While I was learning more about him, I was no closer to knowing who he was or what he was doing with a kid like me. I was still stuck on my first impression, that he might be a molester. I mean, I might have been a hustler just working him for his money, but I'd feel better if I found I were a victim instead of a perpetrator. Being a boy prostitute wasn't exactly appealing.

I needed more clues. What had I missed? Then it hit me. If I couldn't find any evidence to figure him out, what about me? There has to be something of mine in the room. If there wasn't… my thoughts drifted off. If there wasn't any evidence of my presence in his life perhaps I was a prostitute. Maybe he wasn't my boyfriend and maybe I'd only been in his bed for the night.

My clothes!

Who ever I was and who ever I was to him, I sure didn't come here naked. I must have clothes somewhere out there in the bedroom. Maybe I'd find something in my pockets to shed light on the situation.

Walking back into the bedroom I was again stuck by the starkness of the place. There were a few framed pieces of art-work on the walls, landscapes mostly, but all in all it was plain white. I let my eyes roam, looking for my clothing. There were no clothes. The few pieces of furniture with horizontal surfaces were devoid of any clutter. There were those cufflinks, the fra-grances, and the books and trophies, and there was grandpa lying in bed. Beyond that the place didn't look lived in.

I walked around the bed and then the dresser, looking into the corners to see if my clothes were on the floor, hidden by the furniture. They weren't, but something else was. Lying on the rug in the corner where the dresser meets the wall, I noticed a glittering gold ring. I bent down and picked it up. It was a wedding band. It was heavy, thick with gold. Flipping it over in my fingers I tried to remember if I'd ever seen gramps wearing it? Was he married? Was I his down low? I also thought about the cufflinks I'd earlier found and again considered whether or not I should just slip this thing into my pocket, hold on to it in case I needed to use it. If it turned out he was just fucking me, or if I really was paid sex... well, I could hock the ring for a few more bucks when I got back on the streets. And, if it turned out I was more like a call boy and there was a good chance I'd be back here bonking him on other nights, I could simply drop it back on the floor and let him find it on his own. Then again, if instead of just fucking me he was fucking with me, it could become a weapon. I could, at the appropriate time, produce the wedding band, wave it in his face and threaten to tell his wife.

Ok, I decided, the ring goes in my pocket. Now all I got to do is find my clothes and with them, a pocket.

Just about the time I'd decided to keep his wedding band I heard his voice.

"You looking for something?"

I spun around so fast that my towel came undone and fell from my waist. He was sitting up in bed and he asked me again.

"What are you looking for?"

I couldn't think. Maybe if he was awake when I came out of the closet or when I first walked into the room, but he got me just at that moment when I'd decided to steal his ring and quite honestly I felt like a thief.

"Hey," he called to me again, "did you lose something other than your towel?"

Actually, I was so startled by getting caught that I hadn't noticed the loss of my towel until he brought it up. Now I realized I was standing there naked in front of him. I also realized that he wasn't looking at my boy parts. He was looking at my face. He was looking into my eyes.

His eyes were blue, with little wrinkles at each corner that widened into larger wrinkles as they ran down his face. Having just woken up, his face was filled with the stubble of a night's beard growth. His grey hair was stringy and sparse. He wasn't a really attractive man at all. Mostly, you'd just describe him as old. By contrast, I was young. My skin was soft, my muscles tight and my manhood - boyhood - was hanging out in front of him. Why wasn't he looking at it? What was wrong with me?

I grew suddenly angry. Why? Was I angry because he wasn't glued to my precious prick? Was I angry because I'd gotten caught stealing his wedding ring? Careful not to let it fall from my grip, I wrapped myself back in the towel and twisted it snug on my hips.

"I was looking for my clothes," I said letting the anger show in my voice. "Where the hell are they?"

He smiled. "Well, my guess is you folded your pants, placed them on a hanger and hung them over there in the closet. The rest of your things, your shirt, socks and underwear are probably down in the laundry room where you took them after you took them off."

"Excuse me?"

"I said," he repeated, "that if I were putting my money on it, you're clothes are put where they belong, in the closet and in the clothes hamper downstairs in the basement."

"What," with a little less anger in my voice, "I undressed down in the basement and walked back up to your bedroom with nothing on?"

He smiled again.

"Almost."

"Almost what," I asked? "Almost naked?"

The smile left his face. He adopted a serious expression, but not one without some serenity.

"No, you were bare ass buck naked from the basement to the bedroom. It's just that it's not my bedroom," Grandpa revealed.

"So who's is it," I asked"

The smile returned to his face and with it, a warm glow. The lines around his eyes kind of drew together like little arrows that pointed to a sparkle that replaced his pupils.

"It's your room, Chadwick."

This I hadn't expected.

"My room?"

"Yes," he replied as he tossed the sheet and blankets off and put his legs over the edge of the bed.

"This is your room, mine is down the hall." He stood up. "Your clothes are in the laundry room hamper where you always put them, except for your trousers which I have no doubt you'll find hanging in that closet. Your seams will be creased, the zipper front will be facing you and they will hang next to all your other trousers just left of your shirts. Your shoes will sit polished on the floor, neatly paired and placed so they're close but not touching."

"Yeah, so how do you know all this," I questioned him with some suspicion?

"You, my dear son, are a creature of habit," came his reply.

I was confused. Looking around the room I tried to make sense of what he was saying. This was my stuff? This was my room? Was that really my clothing hanging in the closet? When I was checking the labels I should have checked sizes. Just then it stuck me. He had called me his son. It was worse than I had imagined, worse than my worse nightmare could ever have been. I was screwing my own father.

"You sick fuck!" I yelled spinning around to face him again. He was walking toward me now and this time it was his body that was unclothed. It was just as wrinkled as his face and just knowing it belonged to my father turned my stomach.

"You sick, sick fucking bastard," I yelled pushing him away. "Don't touch me you pervert. Don't fucking touch me."

I tried to turn and flee but it was no use. His hands were on my arms, holding me in place. I tugged at his grip but it proved surprisingly strong. The old man must be going to the gym, I thought turning to face him.

"So what now? You gonna rape me? Incest isn't enough?

My dad sat back down on the bed and slowly shook his head. At the same time another smile crossed his wrinkled face. "What are you talking about?"

"I'm talking about you, you incestuous fuck. I'm talking about any man who would even consider sleeping with his son," I shot back.

"My son? His smile now became a little chuckle. "Is that who you think you are, my son?"

"Well," I explained, "that's what you called me. You called me your son."

"No Chadwick, I didn't." He stopped chuckling. Adopting a much more serious look he went on. "I may have used the word son, but it was only used as a term of endearment. You are not my son and I most certainly am not your father."

"Then who the fuck are you?"

"Just calm down, Chad. I'm your lover, your husband or wife or whatever you want to call me this morning. We live together."

"Oh yeah," I said doubtfully, "then how come you said this was my bedroom and yours was down the hall?"

"Because it is," he went on. When you moved in with me I though it would be a much better idea if we kept separate rooms and you agreed."

"Why?"

"Well, for appearances. We've got a significant age difference if you hadn't noticed. Then again, you had been my student. I was afraid that people would talk, that I'd lose my tenure at the University."

Now my mind was fuddled. "Ok, let's go back a bit and start this conversation over. You and I are boyfriends but I don't remember a thing about you. This is my room but I don't recognize any of the furniture. Those are my clothes yet nothing seems to click. It's as if my mind has been wiped clean."

He rose and crossed the room to me. Taking my shoulders with both of his hands and lowering his voice to a soft whisper he said, "You'll just have to trust that what I tell you is true. Your name is Chadwick White... "

"I know my name," I cut him off. It's you I'm not sure of."

"Shhh," he continued his whisper. "My name is David. We've been living together five years. I was your professor but now I'm your lover. This is our house, and this is your bedroom. Everything is just fine, relax."

Again, I looked around the room. "Then how come I can't remember any of this?"

"You get that way sometimes," he answered. "Sometimes you get confused. Sometimes you can't remember things, but I assure you that what I'm telling you is the truth."

I remembered the ring. Holding it out to him, I inquired, "then this isn't yours? You're not married?"

"I am. We are. That is your ring, not mine," he replied.

"I'm married?"

"To me," he said taking the ring and slipping it on my middle finger. It fit.

This time I crossed the room and sat down on the bed. My bed?

"Chadwick," he continued. "You have a condition. Nothing serious, it's just that sometimes you wake up and your memories aren't clear. Sometimes you can't remember where you are or who you are or who I am. There's nothing to be frightened about, in a few moments it will come back to you."

"How do you know?"

His smile came back. "I live with you. I love you. I know all about you and we've been through this a million times."

I was confused. "Let me get this straight. You're my boyfriend, we're married but sometimes I can't remember your name?"

"Exactly. I know it sounds strange to you right now but it's true. Yesterday you called me Robbie all day. The day before it was Richard and you were going on and on about how I'd treated you at a party the night before. It's not serious, you just get confused at times."

"So this is my room and those are my clothes and you're my lover and I'm just confused?"

"Yes, dear."

"Ok," I considered, "what's that you were saying about being my professor. I'm supposed to be your student or some-thing?"

"Were my student," he revealed. "We met at the univer-sity; you were in one of my classes. We were spending a lot of time together, we fell in love and the rest is history."

"Maybe it's history to you, but to me it's just a blank. Why were we spending so much time together, how did we fall in love?

"You were my assistant," he began but again I cut him off.

"I thought you said I was a student?"

"You were. You were a grad student. And, you were very, very intelligent. The university -- well my department head at the university - tapped you to become a teaching assistant and, to my immense delight, you were assigned back to me. We started spending a lot of time together, one thing led to the next, here you are."

By now he'd crossed the room and was sitting next to me on the bed.

"But our age difference," I said. "You're old enough to be my grandfather - my great grandfather - what did we see in each other?"

"Our minds," he replied slipping his arm over my shoul-der. "We fell in love with each other's minds. Chadwick," he looked deep into my eyes as he continued, "Chadwick, I'd never met anyone as intelligent and inquisitive and eager to learn as you were. We spend hours and hours discussing volumes and volumes, and we attended lectures together and went to symposiums together. We had the same interests; the same likes and dislikes, the same minds. We were spending all of our time together..."

I just couldn't help cutting him off, "So then you seduced me?"

He chuckled again. "No, Chad, it was you who seduced me. I wanted you, but I didn't act on my desires. I thought it was wrong, you being a student and me your teacher. No, Chadwick, you seduced me and it was wonderful. I couldn't believe that anyone as beautiful and young and intelligent as you would fall for me, but you did. And, the first night we made love the spell was cast. You showed up at my door the next day with all your belongings. We've lived our lives together every since, never been apart."

I still couldn't remember these things he was telling me. Still, it seemed he was telling the truth. There was something about his manner, his well-worn face, and his eyes. I wanted to trust him. I wanted to believe the things he was saying.

"So, we've never been apart?"

"Well, not physically," he replied. "Your mind, your beautiful, intelligent mind has a few quirks. Sometimes we're apart in your mind. Like this morning, sometimes you can't remember who I am or what you're doing here. It's like you get lost or something, but you always come around, you figure it out."

I tried to make sense of what he was saying. Apparently, if he were to be believed, he was my mate. This old man and I were kick'en it. I'd been living with him for five years but some quirk in my brain wouldn't let me remember.

Look at him, I thought; maybe that's why I don't want to remember. Then I looked down at my hand, at the band of gold now encircling my ring finger. We were married?

"Tell me about this marriage," I demanded. When did we get married? And, what do you mean by marriage?

"We were married in a civil ceremony in Toronto, shortly after you heard that Canada was recognizing gay unions. You'd been researching it at work. One day you came home all excited and bubbling about our ability to really get married, legal and everything. You said you wanted to do it and we were on the next plane north. There's a certificate hanging downstairs in the dining room," he said with total believability.

"It was my idea to get married," I asked?

"Yes, just as it was your idea for us to move in together. Actually our entire physical relationship has been your idea. At first I fought you. I didn't think it was proper, what with our age difference and all."

"You fought me? I was the one pushing this relation-ship?"

"Yes," he admitted. "If it weren't for your absolute belief in us I don't think it would have happened. But you did believe, and your persistence overcame my reservations. I might add," he said placing his hand on my naked knee, "I'm absolutely and totally happy you kept the pressure on me. You've been the best thing that's ever happened to me and I wouldn't want anything to ever change."

I looked doubtful. "How about my mental thing," I asked?

He smiled again. "You mean the blank spots? No, I guess I wouldn't even change that. I've grown used to you and your various quirks."

"Various? You mean there are more," I inquired somewhat hesitant to hear his answer.

"Oh, nothing to cause concern. Some of them even make life easier for me."

"Like what," I demanded.

"Well," he said pausing to think a moment. "Well, there's your compulsion to clean. Our house sparkles. You could literally eat off the floors. Just look around you. Everything has its place and everything is in its place. You see to that. That's how I knew that you would have hung your trousers and put the rest of your dirty clothes in the hamper."

"What else?"

"Hmm, I'm not sure I should bring it up... "

"Bring it," I told him. "I want to know it all."

"Ok, here's one of the things you do," he said earnestly. "Sometimes, particularly in the mornings when you first wake up, you experience flash backs or something. I'm not sure what to call them, but it's like you're living another life. Sometimes you call me by other names. Sometimes you insist that you've done things I know you couldn't possibly have done. And every once in awhile your just, well... different."

"Like how," I asked?

"The things you do," he answered.

"What things?"

"Sex," he replied. "Sexually you're just different. You're more animated, inquisitive, and experimental, it changes each time. It's difficult to explain it, but it's the things that you do."

"And what do you do?"

"I enjoy you," he replied through a smile. "I really enjoy you."

There was something in that smile. I still didn't know if what he was telling me was true, not from my own independent knowledge. But I did know that I trusted him. I can't say why, but I felt secure with him. His arm was still draped over my shoulder and now he pulled me to him and rested his head on my own.

"You know," he told me, "I love you. I respect your intellect. I admire your energy. I think you're an incredible man and I just simply love you."

His pronouncement made me feel good. I believed him. I wanted to believe him. I wanted to be loved and I wanted that love to come from him. How strange is that, I asked myself? I don't really know this man, not really. The only things I know about him are the things he's just told me. And yet, I want him to love me. I want what he's saying to be true.

"You said there was something else," I prompted.

"What?"

"You said there was something else," I repeated.

"I don't know what you mean," he replied.

"You were telling me some of my strange behaviors and you said, "Here's one of the things you do." That would imply that there are other things I do. What things?

"Ahh," he said, pausing a moment as if to think. "So you want the full story do you?"

His other arm came up, crossed my chest and his two hands clasped. He held me in a loose hug.

"Ok, here it goes," he began. "Sometimes, when you first wake up, you think you're a different person."

"I know that, at least I know that you just told me I do."

"Yes," he continued, "but what I haven't told you is that most of the time - well, all of the time really - you can't seem to remember who I am."

"You mean like now?"

"Exactly. Just like now. I have to tell you who I am and you have to ask me a lot of questions. Slowly, it just seems to click and you accept my statements and our day begins. But, you never really admit that you know that what I've said is the truth. At least you apparently never know it on your own. You only accept what I've told you and act on it."

This was getting very strange. I took what he was telling me and mulled it over in my mind.

"So it's sort of like amnesia or something. I mean, if I never have any independent memories of you, of our life together, and you have to tell me about it everyday, that's amnesia isn't it," I inquired?

"I guess so," he answered. Then he turned to face me. Taking my chin in his hand he turned my head so that we were looking at each other. Face to face, his breath mingling with mine, he began. In a soft, reassuring voice he began.

"David Dupree', do you take this man, Chadwick White, to be your lawfully wedded spouse. Do you promise to love him in sickness and in health, for richer for poorer, in good times as well as bad, until the last breath of your body and death do you part?"

He answered his own question, "I do." Then, squeezing me in his arms he continued, "And Chadwick White, do you take David to be your lawfully wedded spouse. Do you promise to love him in sickness and in health, for richer for poorer, in good times as well as in bad, until the last breath of your body and death do you part?"

He didn't have to answer. I looked into his eyes, felt his big, strong arms holding me, I swear that I actually felt his soul as I said, "I do. I most certainly do."

He kissed me. It was a warm, passionate kiss that lasted a full minute. At least it seemed that way. And during that kiss I let myself fall into him, the essence of whom or what I was fell deeper and deeper into the essence of this man. I didn't care that he was three times my age. I no longer saw his wrinkles or his thinning hair. I felt him, and what I felt was strong and reassuring. I believed him, and I believed that we were deeply in love.

I wish that feeling could have lasted. I really wanted it to go on and on, but it didn't. After a minute or so I pushed him away.

"Wait a minute," I protested. "You're saying my brain is all scrambled, that I'm crazy or something."

"No, not at all," said that same calm and reassuring voice. "You've got one of the most brilliant minds I've ever known. I told you, that's why were together. I admire and adore you, but it's your brilliant mind that holds us together. We don't communicate over a generational divide. When it comes to intellect, we're on the same level. It's true; you have a few quirks, but nothing I can't live with and nothing that you can't handle. We handle it together."

"So I'm not crazy."

"You're crazy in love with me. At least I hope so. And, I'm crazy in love with you too."

He released me from his embrace and gently pushed me to my feet. A quick flip of his fingers released the towel from around my waist and exposed my ass to him. He slapped it.

"You'd better get dressed; you'll be late for work."

The sting of his hand on the smooth, round skin of my butt cheeks felt good. It woke me a little and helped snap my mind into place. I felt compelled to move, to get dressed and to get to my job. I didn't even know what my job was, but I knew that I couldn't be late. I knew that I never arrived late. Apparently, I had the obsessive-compulsive disorder and among my compulsions was the need to be on time. The sting of his slap on my posterior had jiggled my brain and several things fell into place. The room became familiar. It was my room. I recognized the furnishings, recognized my awards, and I remembered every one of my precious, precious books. I

knew where my clothes were, what was in every drawer.
There was no doubt what I'd wear, and I set about selecting
those garments.

Now, I know this must sound strange to you and I admit
that it seems strange to me, but at the same time, it felt very
right. It felt like my life. Its familiarity was reassuring, like
something that happens every day, a routine. I thought about
this all day, and I thought about David. I didn't really remember
much about him, not our daily existence anyway. The only two
memories I had were from this morning. My thoughts were
filled with the sight of him sitting on the bed, holding me, his
eyes looking into mine, his strong embrace. I listened to his
voice again in my mind.

My other memory was of our wedding. That memory
was fresh and filled with details. It wasn't just the vows he'd
repeated this morning. I could see every detail in my brain. I
knew what we were wearing and where we had stayed. Every
detail of the hotel room, every detail of the courthouse, every
detail of our wedding was etched in my brain. More importantly, I knew without doubt that I loved him.

As much as my life was coming back to me, there were
still some blanks. Occasionally a total stranger would come up
to me and begin talking as if we were old friends. I didn't know
them from Adam but they sure knew me. Each time it took
several seconds before the memories of them and of what ever
we had been working on came back. Eventually I'd realize that
they weren't really strangers, but co-workers. Twice, when I
left my office, I had trouble returning to it. I couldn't remember
where it was or what I'd been doing. On each of these occa-
sions I tried a trick to jog my memory. I can't say how I knew it
would work, but each time I blanked out I called on the
strongest memory I could recall. I conjured up David's image,
sitting on the bed this morning, assuring me that everything

was all right.

He was obviously an important figure in my life, a strong influence, and a protector. I couldn't wait to finish work and get home to him, to rediscover our life together. When, at last, five o'clock came and I finished work, I thought about him all the way home. I didn't have much choice. See, when I checked out of work and left the building I couldn't remember which way to turn. Literally! I didn't know to go left; I didn't know to go right. At first I was frightened, but then David popped up in my mind and I sensed that turning left was correct. Two blocks later I was confronted with six busses waiting for passengers at the terminal. I absolutely remembered that I needed to board one of these busses but which one was uncertain. David, David, David, I repeated his name silently under my breath. Before long one of the busses seemed right, and it was. I got on, picked out a seat and sat back for the ride home.

Home - Now there's something I remembered. Home was where David was and where I'd be safe. Looking out the window I took in a very nice city, but not a city I remembered. Each building was a new sight to me, each street name a new name. I didn't worry. I was no longer frightened. It must be like this a lot in my life, I thought, and I'm still here. However I've managed to make it, I've managed. With David's help, both physically and mentally, I've managed to overcome this strange affliction and I'll be fine now. I'm going to make it home. I'm going to return to David. Still, the fact that my confidence was strong didn't change one thing. Mine was a very strange mind. I was caught in a very weird life.

The bus eventually reached my block, our block - David's and mine - and I got off. There was our house, our big old beautiful house. There was my sanctuary, my womb. I hurried inside.

As I walked through the door everything fell into place. I knew where the mail would be and picked it up. I sorted through the envelopes, knowing to put the bills in the top drawer of the small table standing in the vestibule. Most of the letters were for David and I knew that he wanted me to stack them on the corner of the counter in the kitchen. Upstairs, I stripped from my work clothes, carefully creased the pants and took them into the closet - my closet. I hung them to the left of my shirts, making sure the zipper front was facing me. Once hung, I adjusted them two or three times so they were centered on the hanger and not touching any of the other trousers on either side. I walked back to the bedroom, retrieved my shoes and placed them in the closet too. I remembered to place them close to my other shoes, but not touching. I hung up my tie and then gathered everything else I'd been wearing and carried it all to the basement.

I found myself folding each piece of clothing before placing it into the hamper next to the washing machine. It made me laugh. Damn, I told myself, I'm pretty screwed up. I even folded my socks. Then slipping out of my jockey shorts, I placed them - folded of course - on the top of the pile. Standing there naked, feeling the cool of the basement on my skin, I was free.

Half way up the basement stairs I heard the door open and knew instinctively that David was home. I couldn't wait to see him, to tell him about my bizarre day. Taking the steps two at a time, I burst into the kitchen just as he was picking up his mail. He wasn't surprised to see me. Apparently, even my lack of clothing was expected.

"Hey boy," he greeted me, "how was your day."

"You wouldn't believe it," I answered. "I got lost all day."

"Oh, I'd believe you. You get lost every day. But, if I can take a guess, you fixed your mind on me and things just started making sense."

"Yes," I said slightly amazed. That's exactly what I did. How did you know?"

"Because," he replied placing his arms around me. "That's what you do everyday." Then he kissed me. It was a deep, passionate kiss. And, it felt just right.

"Come on," he said pulling me into the hall, "lets go up stairs and make love."

"Now?"

"Yup," he said knowingly. "We do that everyday too."

After our love making finished we both took showers. He went to his bathroom, I went to mine. His was tiled in blue with photos in frames on the walls. His towels were black and matched the rug on the floor. My bathroom was white, stark white. I remembered it, and it felt right. After our showers, and after we'd redressed, I cooked him supper. We ate in the dining room then retired to the library for coffee.

In any other house our "library" would have been called the living room or parlor. But, in our home the walls were covered in shelves and the shelves were filled with books. It felt warm and cozy and very safe. We sat there for the rest of the evening. I told David about the less strange parts of my day, the projects I'd been researching, and the assignments I'd completed. He told me about a lecture he'd attended and about a new student who'd transferred into his class mid-term. But mostly we talked about us. I wanted to know everything.

David obliged. He described our courtship, the places we'd gone and the people we knew. He laid out our lives together and as he did the pieces began coming together and fitting just fine. I knew that what he was telling me was true. I knew that this man was my man and always would.

"David," I asked an hour or two into the conversation, "I'm curious about something."

"What's that?"

"Is it always like this," I wondered?

"Like what?"

"Am I always lost? Are there any days when I just remember everything, like who you are and who I am and what the fuck is going on in my life?"

"Sure, most of the time," he replied.

"You mean I'm not always this mentally ill?"

"Whoa boy," he put my brakes on. "We don't call you mentally ill, you're not. You have periods of insecurity; times when you're confused and need some reassurance, but you sure as hell aren't crazy if that's what you're asking."

"It seems like I am," I replied. Then I started to cry.

David slipped from the chair he was sitting in and sat down on the floor by my feet. He began to stroke my legs and talk to me in low tones.

"Chad, you've had a difficult life. Most people who have gone through the things you have would have shut down a long time ago. Lots of them might have cash in their chips. But not you, you're strong. You've got a brilliant mind and great reasoning. There are sometimes when you depend upon me to hold it together, like today for instance. But even during these episodes you're reasonable. You don't freak out, and as time goes by these episodes get fewer and fewer in frequency."

"My life has been difficult?," I asked him.

"To say the least," he answered. "Yours was a very difficult childhood, and after that it didn't get much better. You were a mess when I first met you. College helped, and as we grew closer we spent a great deal of time working on the situation and ironing things out."

I searched my mind. Even though our discussion had brought many of my memories to the front of my brain, I couldn't recall any part of my life before David. My childhood was a blank. I wanted to ask David about it, but I was afraid to know. Better to just trust him and accept that there was a good reason I was the way I was.

"I'm afraid, David," I confessed. "It seems like I can't trust my life, like there is nothing constant at all.

"Oh my Chad," David replied pulling me a little closer. "Let me tell you one of the great truths of life. There is nothing constant but change. Even people who think they have it made; people who think they have their lives all tied up in a neat little bundle; even those people are just deluding themselves. Things can change in an instant. A car comes out of nowhere and suddenly your husband's dead, a fire bursts out in the middle of the night and your home and all your possessions are gone. You go to the doctor to check out that little cough and he tells you your dying."

Now David looked me in the eyes, "Chad, nothing about life is really secure. What you've got to do, what we all have to do, is make the most of today. You need to be the best you can be, regardless of the circumstances you find yourself. Most of all, strive to be happy."

Somehow I knew that I'd always remember what David had just told me, though our conversation drifted to other subjects.

We talked about politics and current affairs. We mulled over the newspaper and even discussed sports. I was surprised at the breath and depth of our interests. David was smart and I was smart, together we seemed to have something to say about almost everything. And, while we talked late into the night, we didn't spend any more time talking about us or about my condition. At least not until very late, just before I nodded off to sleep.

"David," I whispered taking his hand in mine, "doesn't it bother you when I forget who you are?"

He looked at me. The corners of his lips curved upward and formed a little smile. The little lines near the corners of his eyes were still there but I hardly noticed them. He didn't look old to me now. All I could see was his warmth and affection. All I could feel was his love and devotion. And, as he spoke, everything felt fine.

"It doesn't bother me at all. I always know who you are. You're Chadwick White. You're my boyfriend and my best friend. You've brought meaning to my life and given me more joy than any man could desire. I knew who you were before I slipped your ring on my finger and I knew that I wanted to love you for the rest of my life when I slipped my ring on your finger. My life with you has never bothered me, not then, not now, not ever. I love you, Chadwick White, and I trust that you'll always love me."

Leaning down to press his lips against mine his smile became a kiss. It was his kiss, it was my kiss, it was ours.

Our mouths finally parted and I looked at him, "I do love you, David. I do."

He stroked my hair and repeated his love for me several more times before suggesting we move upstairs and go to sleep. It's late, he had said, and he reminded me that I needed to be up early tomorrow for work.

"I don't want to go to sleep," I protested. "I'm afraid."

"How can you be afraid? After all that we've talked about you should be feeling fairly secure?"

"Not about everything," I confessed. "I'm afraid that if I go to sleep I won't wake up next to you in the morning."

A frown took the place where his smile just had been.

"You always wake up next to me," he said shaking his head.

"No, David. No I don't. You don't understand. In the morning you'll be someone else and I don't want to lose you, not ever again."

David dismissed my protests and repeatedly assured me that he wasn't going anywhere that he'd be at my side when the morning came. He sounded convincing, and I believe that he believed himself. I never did. I loved him. I trusted him, but I also believed as surely as I believed that the morning would come that when it did I wake up with someone else. There'd be a new boyfriend in my bed.

CHAPTER FOUR
Thursday

I didn't open my eyes when the alarm went off. I was afraid. This morning my mind wasn't blank. I remembered David, remembered every word of our conversation last evening, and I remembered what had caused my fear as I slipped into sleep. He wasn't going to be next to me. My man, the man I depended upon and who kept me sane wasn't going to be the man I saw if I opened my eyes.

I could feel his body lying close to me; feel the warmth of his skin as it touched mine. I could hear him breathing, but I knew without looking that it wouldn't be David breathing.

Slowly slipping my hand under the sheets I touched that skin and he stirred. Quickly, I pulled my hand back. I didn't want to wake him anymore than I wanted to wake up myself. Instead, I turned away and lifted my lids.

The room that I saw wasn't our room. A second bed stood a few feet away; separated from the one I was in by a nightstand. On that nightstand I could see a small lamp, under it sat a black book and a phone. Reaching over, I snapped on the lamp and slid the book closer so I could see what it was. Embossed in gold lettering on the leather were two words, Holy Bible. Picking it up, I opened the cover and thumbed past the first two pages. There, on the cover sheet I found two more words, Giddien Society.

Sitting up, I looked around the rest of the room. Cheap

framed prints and a generic television hung from the walls. One wall was filled with a window, or so I assumed as the drapery which covered it was pulled tightly closed. The other side of the room opened into an alcove. A long marble counter dominated the alcove with a sink set in, and above the sink a mirror filled the wall. There was a door next to the counter. It was shut. Still, I knew if I opened it I'd find a toilet and I had to pee like a proverbial racehorse.

Quietly I got out of bed, careful not to wake the man I knew wasn't David. I moved silently around the second bed, making my way into the alcove and opened the door. As expected, a toilet greeted me. Standing there, dick in hand, I let loose a stream so strong I was sure the splashing sound would wake up the dead. It didn't. I didn't even wake Sleeping Beauty out there in the room. Still being cautious however, I silently shut the toilet's lid but didn't flush. He hadn't heard my piss but why take chances.

I was tired, terribly tired. For a moment I considered a cold splash of water on my face. That would wake me. But I abandon the thought, not wanting to take the chance of waking him with the noise. I crept back into the room. Unlike private houses, hotel construction is heavy duty, the floor never squeaked as I moved around the bed so I could get a look at him.

As expected, he wasn't David.

He was handsome; I'd guess maybe thirty-five. He wore his dark black hair cropped short, in a flattop. Either he hadn't shaved for a few days or he was doing the goatee thing. There were clothes folded neatly on the other bed and I crossed over to them to take a look. One set included blue jeans, a button down sports shirt and a pair of white crew socks. On the floor I could see a pair of white running shoes that I assumed went with this pile. Next to it was a pair of dress pants, a white shirt and a tie. Across the room, hanging from the back of a chair, hung a navy blue suit coat. Black oxfords were on the floor. Hmmm, thought I, is he the blue jeans or the business suit?

Again, I silently crossed the room and picked up the suit coat. Sliding my hand into the inner pocket, I felt for a wallet or papers or anything that might give me a clue. What I found was a small leather case containing a stack of business cards. Taking one out, I read the name, Richard Rassmussen, Attorney-at-Law.

I don't always know who my man is in the morning. Sometimes my mind is devoid of the details of our lives. But I always know who I am. Never once have I opened my eyes and not been Chadwick White. My boyfriend behind me in bed must be Richard Rassmussen, Attorney-at-Law. I returned the card to the stack and slipped the case back into his pocket. What else could I ascertain?

I went back to the piles of clothes on the unoccupied and unused bed. If the suit coat was his, so were the dress pants. I found a wallet in the back pocket. Inside the wallet was the usual array of credit cards and quite a bit of cash. A driver's license confirmed his age, thirty-seven. Pretty close, I thought, congratulating myself on my ability to guess. He was six foot one, weighed 180 pounds, and when he eventually opened his eyes I now knew that they would be blue.

I put the wallet back into his pocket. Clearly the other pile of clothing belonged to me. They were Hilfiger jeans and they were tight. I had trouble getting them on and I had trouble getting the zipper pulled up. For a moment I considered that perhaps I was wrong, maybe these weren't my pants. But once zipped, I understood why I wore them so tight. My package was huge and these jeans left nothing to the imagination.

Across the room I could see my reflection in the alcove mirror. I looked good, damn good. Turning a half turn, I confirmed that my ass looked as good as the shit I was packing up front.

I enjoyed looking at myself, and why not? Look at me, I thought running my hand over my backside, I was hot. Turning back, I paid equal attention to my crotch. It looked equally hot. Somehow I managed to shove my hand inside the tight confines and adjusted everything to its best advantage then I looked again. Damn hot, I observed.

I didn't bother to put on my shirt. I liked the way the ripples running down my stomach looked. No sense hiding that.

Convinced that my body was beautiful, I decided it was time to find out whether Richard Rassmussen, Attorney-at-Law deserved to have spent the night next to it. I crossed the room to his side of the bed and sat down.

There are a thousand ways to wake someone sleeping. I could clear my throat, make some sort of noise and stir him out of slumber. A backrub makes another gentle way to wake up. I could slap his ass and shock him from sleep. And, if I were more certain of the relationship I had with this man, I might have climbed under the blankets and simply sucked his dick. What a wonderful way to wake him, get his dick up first and the rest of his body will follow. But this morning I wasn't so sure of our status. The only thing I knew of the man beside me was his profession, that and his vital statistics. In the end, I asked a stupid question.

"You awake yet?"

The attorney's eyes opened and he looked up at me. It took him a moment to move. He seemed to be confused; like he had no more an idea of who I was that I had of him. Then his expression cleared and his lips parted in a smile.

"Good morning," he croaked then cleared his throat. "How long have you been awake?"

"Just got up," I lied. "I was just about to jump into the shower."

I couldn't help noticing that his eyes moved down my body and were now locked on my carefully arranged crotch. He reached out and grabbed what he had been staring at.

"You'll have to get out of these first," he laughed pulling me closer and pressing his face where his hand had been. I didn't protest. This felt natural, like it was supposed to be. Gyrating my hips, I pressed myself hard against his face. He pressed harder. I grabbed the back of his head and pulled it into me; he grabbed my ass and pulled back. Richard Rassmussen, Attorney-at-Law, was doing his best to eat me through my jeans. I wasn't stopping him, I was getting aroused.

He mumbled something but I couldn't make it out. He face was pressed so tight against my crotch that what ever he said was mumbled and I couldn't hear. I released my grip so he could pull his mouth away and talk. He didn't release me. Nevertheless, he tried speaking again.

"What?" I still couldn't understand a word he said. That's when he released my butt cheeks and, tilting his head to face mine said, this time quite distinctly, "How about I get up and take that shower with you?"

How could I say no? Why would I? By this time the erection was straining inside the tight confines of my jeans. It was begging to come out in the open and a shower sounded like the perfect opportunity.

"Sure baby," I replied and led him up and out of bed, across the room and through the alcove. In route, I couldn't help looking again in the mirror. Damn it Chadwick, I thought, you do look good.

I stripped out of my jeans and underwear. He was already naked, having slept that way. His member had grown as hard as my own and we stood there a moment admiring each other. Damn, I thought again, we're both pretty hot. As I reached for the shower knob he reached for mine and we stepped laughing into the stall.

When the hot water strikes it usually stirs my memories. The water washes my brain as well as my body clean and I can think again. Long before the shower ends I usually have a pretty good picture of who my boyfriend is and what I'm doing here with him. That's how it happened this morning. Of course it didn't hurt that he started giving me verbal clues. As he picked up the soap and started to rub it on me he asked, "Are we still on the clock?"

"Say what?" I didn't know what he meant.

"I'm just wondering if this is still costing money?"

Just as he said it my brain flashed and a bright white light, almost like a flash bulb, went off in my head. This time there was no question, no second-guessing or doubt of mind. This time, clear as crap I knew what the situation was - prostitution.

"Sure," I replied. "Just like always."

He didn't seem phased. He wasn't shocked or even dismayed. In fact, he didn't miss a beat, but continued to soap my body, using the occasion to run his hands all over it. When he got to the best part it was ready, willing and able. Firmly erect, it got harder as he wrapped his hands around it.

My first thought was that I'd ejaculated. The sensations that wracked my body caused me to quiver and my muscles tensed. I arched my back. My lips tightened and my head was thrown back. But, I didn't cum. Instead, I kind of went. The "out-of-body" portion of this shower had clearly begun.

I found myself standing on a street corner. It was night and the pavement was wet. Had it been raining? A pool of light illuminated the corner, but everything else was black. I wasn't alone. A short distance from me another guy stood, hands shoved into his pockets. He was glancing up and down the street. I tried to see what he was looking for but basically the street was empty. About half a block away another pool of light shone down and another guy was standing under it.

Shortly, a car drove by, a dark green Lincoln. It slowed and the driver looked directly at me, then he continued on up the street turning left at the following corner. Obviously, I thought, I'm not so alone as it appears.

A few minutes later another car turned onto our street about two blocks away. As it approached the guy half a block down, the driver slowed then came to a stop. The man standing there leaned into the passenger window and they exchanged a few words. At least that's what I assume happened. I was too far away to know for sure. What I did know was that the driver leaned over then opened the passenger door and the guy on the street slid in. The car started up and in moments was passing my corner, right under my street light. As it did, I couldn't help recognizing it. It was the same car that had just passed and checked me out. The same dark green

Lincoln.

The car with its new passenger drove up the street and continued out of sight. Now there were two people left standing on the street, me and the man to my side, the man with his hands shoved in his pockets. He said something. It was under his breath so I couldn't hear. It was like he was grumbling or something. I looked in his direction. Shortly, he removed his hands from his pockets, turned and walked away. Half a block later he was standing under the lamp where the last guy got picked up.

It was cold and I turned up my collar to the biting wind. A few more cars drove by. Each time, the driver slowed and looked at us, me and the guy down the street. Each time the car picked up speed and continued. Eventually one stopped and the guy down the street got in. Now I really was alone.

Someone said something that startled me. I wasn't expecting to hear anything but the wind yet someone's voice was speaking to me from a few inches away. Spinning my head around to see who it was, I was instantly transported back to the motel and into the shower. Richard Rassmussen, Attorney-at-Law was standing there naked as a jaybird and with a quizzical look on his face.

"Earth to Chadwick," he said and I knew those were the words I'd just heard. "Earth to Chadwick," he repeated, "are you there?"

"Huh?"

"I'm wondering where you were? Its like you just drifted away," he said in an impatient way.

Realizing that my mind had wondered I searched for an

excuse. "Sorry," I stammered, "guess I got lost in the moment. You feel so good. Come here and kiss me." I pulled him close and our lips met. Streams of water cascaded over us and his hands resumed their exploration across my back and down to the crack in my ass. His fingers probed there as his tongue dipped down my throat. Leaning back, I relaxed and closed my eyes. He really did feel good and I really did lose myself in that moment.

When I opened my eyes again the shower was gone. I was still lip locked in a passionate embrace but the man with his tongue curled around mine wasn't Richard Rassmussen. This guy was older. His shirt was off but he still wore the rest of his clothes. And, while we were not in the shower, his body was wet and slippery, just like Richard's had been.

The new man was slightly overweight and covered with sweat. From the way he was breathing I could tell he was into me and what we were doing. I could also tell he was a heavy smoker. His breathing came heavy and you could hear a wheeze in each gasp. The air coming out of his lungs also reeked of stale nicotine, that and alcohol. He wasn't real old, just out of condition.

I would have asked myself what in the fuck I was doing with this man but the answer was obvious. His hands fumbled with the front of his pants and moments later they were down near his ankles. A few moments more and he was out of his shorts, naked and bare. Following suit, I removed my clothes and pressed myself to him, letting his sweat lubricate my skin. Turning my head from the smell of his breath, I let him slide down my body and do what he did. Just get it over with, I thought. I didn't like him with his cigarettes and stink and sweat. If only he were Richard Rassmussen, I thought, Attorney-at-Law.

Maybe the man made me cum, or maybe it was just the fact that I was thinking of Richard, I don't know. What I do know is that just as I was wishing the fat sweaty guy were gone, replaced by Richard - just when I wanted my attorney - my wish came true. I found myself back standing in the shower with water, not sweat, running down my stomach. Following the current as it washed past my navel and through the thick tangle of my pubic hair, I smiled. The lips I saw sliding up and down my dick belonged to Richard Rassmussen, the man I'd found sleeping in my motel room bed.

By now you're probably thinking that I really am crazy. I mean, I woke up wanting Richard to be David and I'd been calling David by Robbie's name when I was with him. You'd think I would settle my mind on one boyfriend, that my desire for stability would lock me on one train of thought. But it's not like that, not at all. For me, security and stability rests in my ability to keep one man in the forefront of my mind each day - the man I found sleeping in my bed each day when I woke. Right now, that man was Richard -- Richard Rassmussen, Attorney-at-Law. And right now, as I looked down, he was the man with my manhood ramming in and out of his mouth.

"Take it, Richard! Take it all, bastard," I said as forcefully as I could.

"What did you call me," he asked as he spit me from his lips.

His hair was too short to wrap my fingers around so I grabbed at his ears. Shoving his face back where it belonged, I called him a bastard once more. My grip was firm and this time my dick choked out any protest he might make.

How many times do you think you can cum? I don't mean in your entire life, just in one day. That's the thought that was crossing my mind as a new blast shot out and I threw my head back with a shout. I could do this over and over and over again, if he'd keep doing what he had been doing. Instead, I felt him let me slip from his lips and looked down. I should have been shocked to see that those lips didn't belong to Richard, but I wasn't. They didn't even belong to the fat guy. No, it didn't shock me at all to find that the man spitting my juice onto the floor was a stranger. Weren't they all?

This stranger stood up and wiped his face with the sleeve of his shirt. Fuck, I thought, he didn't even get undressed. I found my own pants crumpled around my ankles and pulled them up. I was still fastening my belt when I realized he was half out the door. Wham, bam, thank you man, I thought as I looked around for my shirt. No grass would grow under this guy's feet. I heard the door close and he was gone. Sure hope I was paid in advance.

Prostitution fit me well. You don't have ties to a hustler. Like this last one, the men just come and go -- No pun intended. And, there was no shame in the world's oldest profession, at least not for me. The men in my life come and go every day. This way at least I get paid. As I opened the door to walk out myself, I shoved my hands into my pockets - empty! I patted my back pockets then turned and looked around the room. Shit! No money! I hadn't been paid in advance.

Walking back out into the bright light of day, I heard the door close behind me then open again.

"Hey! Where you going? We're paid in full for the rest of the day." I turned around. Richard Rassmussen stood holding the door open.

"Just running down to the lobby to see if I can score some coffee," I said with a smile. "Don't get dressed. I'll be right back for a second go round." What the hell, I said to myself, it was his dime. Like I told you, there was not a limit in my ability to perform.

The difference between street hustlers and call boys rests in the price they charge, they're both whores. Some take up the profession because they're oversexed, others just need the attention. I had no idea why I engaged in the practice. I simply woke up this way this morning. I did like it a lot. I was certainly oversexed, at least so it would seem. I couldn't get the thought of returning to Richard out of my mind. By the time I returned to the room from the lobby I'd spilled most of the coffee I was bringing back to him. Still, the two cups were occupying both of my hands so I "knocked" on the door with my foot.

You can imagine my surprise when the door to the room opened. It wasn't my attorney friend standing there, but yet another trick. This one was already undressed and, from the state of his manhood, apparently waiting for me.

"Come in, I've been waiting for you," he said with a thick Southern drawl. He had a football player's body with muscles rippling everywhere and I couldn't help taking a few seconds to stare. There wasn't a hair on him from his head to his toe. He'd even shaved his pubes that only served to make his huge standing member look larger.

"Well," I said sucking my breath in, "here I am now and you seem like you're ready." I stepped through the threshold, my heart skipping a beat in rampant anticipation.

This guy was good. Living up to his football player appearance, he tackled me, ripped my jeans off and carried me to the bed. Now, I'm not a small fellow. I'm six feet if I'm an inch and while my weight didn't match his, no one would call me small. In his arms I was nothing - no weight at all. I relaxed and let him take me, not just to the bed but in all ways sexually too. Our lovemaking took hours. He was more sexed than I, and he emptied himself inside me numerous times in numerous places. I wanted it to go on all day, though I must admit I was getting somewhat worried that I couldn't keep the performance going. Still, I probably needed the money, the last time I checked my pockets they had been empty. That's when I looked across the room. There, to my great surprise, were Richard's clothes still folded on the bed.

This was getting strange. Not like my whole life isn't strange, but never before had my men - or evidence of them - overlapped like this. That is if you don't count calling Richard, Robbie or things like that. I didn't know what to think of finding Richard's clothes still in the room but I hoped like hell his wallet was there too.

"What you looking at, boy," the football player said cupping my chin in his hand and forcefully turning my gaze away from Richard's clothes. He squeezed his fingers and pinched my face together so hard that it hurt. "You're with me now, boy. I get your full and undivided attention. Understand?"

If I didn't understand, I soon would. His pounding resumed with more passion and force than before as he filled me yet another time. When he finished with me we were both spent and exhausted. I fell back on the bed and passed out. When I finally woke up he was gone.

I nearly broke my leg falling out of bed in my rush to Richard's pants. Good as he had been, if that football playing faggot had ripped me off I'd kill him. Forget that I didn't know his name or even how he'd hired me, if that wallet wasn't there, or if it were empty, I'd kill him.

My fears were unfounded. The wallet was still in Richard's pocket, its contents safe and sound. The money had not been taken and there were plenty of credit cards though I wasn't sure how many there were supposed to have been. I breathed a sign of relief before heading to the showers. The game had been exhaustive and my body needed to be revived.

I stepped into the stall, twisted the knob and closed my eyes as hot streams of water shot out and splashed off my face. It felt good. So had the football player, I thought as I lost myself in the memory of past few hours. Every inch of my body was sore, inside and out. The pulsating jets of hot water were doing their best to relax my aching muscles and I gave myself over to their assault. I could have stayed in that shower all day but the phone started ringing out in the room and the sound jolted me back to my senses. Naked and dripping I ran to answer it.

"Hello," I said into the receiver.

"Hey, baby," came the reply. "I was wondering if we're hooking up today?"

"Who is this," I inquired?

"Who the fuck do you think it is," he said. "I know you're a busy man but you've seen me every Thursday for the past three years."

"Just kidding," I said into the phone, though I wasn't. I didn't want to tell him I had no idea who he was. Obviously he was one of my regulars though, and I didn't think I should piss him off. "Of course we're kicking it today, just tell me when and where and I'll be there. You've got a friend."

"I'll come to you," his voice said in the earpiece. "It'll be 'bout an hour, you still in the same hotel?"

I cupped the receiver and crossed the room, stretching the cord to its limit. Opening the door I checked the number, "Yes, room 121."

"Cool, baby, be ready for me. I'm horny as hell and can't wait to see you."

"Mmm," I replied, "me too!" I heard the click of the phone on his end then replaced my own handset in its cradle. Maybe there was a limit to the number of times I could do it. I guess I was going to find out. Then I walked back through the alcove and into the still running shower.

When the knock on the door came I was laying on the bed. The shower had done wonders for my recovery, but I still felt drained. Stretched out and clad only in underwear, I was drifting in and out of sleep and at first thought the knock was part of a dream. The knock came again.

I glanced at the clock. An hour and ten minutes had gone by since the last phone call; my regular customer was no doubt the cause of the noise at the door. Rising, I made my way there now, turned the knob and pulled on it to let him in. To say I was shocked by the man waiting to enter would be wrong. I was more than shocked, I was dumfounded. This guy looked to be 17 or so, hardly out of high school. This was my regular, I questioned? What's he doing hiring hookers, he could be working himself, I thought. Still, I swung the door wide open and welcomed him in. What luck I was having, sex with a hot young thing and I'd be getting paid too.

He was all smiles and his smiles were perfect. A bright white and very wide grin stretched from ear to ear. A large shock of curly blonde hair stuck out from under his baseball cap that he wore turned backwards on his head. He was slim and his stomach was flat. A pair of tight, white Levis hugged his hips and left nothing to the imagination as to his endowment. I ushered him in and, as I did, I couldn't help notice his bubble butt backside. Holy shit, he sure looked inviting. I reached out, placed my hand on it and squeezed. My only thought; please God; let him be a bottom so I can pop this bubble.

"Hey, Chad," the boy said and his grin widened. "I was missing you." With that, the boy threw his arms around my neck and planted his moist full lips on mine. I kissed him back, using the opportunity to run my own hands around him and slide them down to that butt. His lips parted and a smooth, silky tongue probed me for mine. He smelled sweet. Fresh and young and eager, what a change from my last four or five customers, I thought. And, this one is a regular to boot.

There are a million reasons why someone will hire a hooker. Sometimes they're old and ugly and the only sex they'll ever get is the sex they buy. Sometimes they're just busy, Richard Rassmussen, Attorney-at-Law, was probably one of those. Their work was so demanding that they just didn't have time to date or even go out to the bars picking up tricks. You wouldn't believe how many married men are on the down low, paying to get their partners to do what their wives won't. And, sometimes the customer is just too damn old and tired and just wants his dick sucked. This boy didn't appear to be any of these types. Maybe he was just into professionals; we do give the best in bed after all. I mean, I don't want to brag or anything but if you want the job done right you need experience. If you're lucky you'll find it, but if you want to be sure then you hire it. Given the amount of experience I'd gained in this one day alone, I figure I must be about as good as it gets. For whatever reason he chooses to pay, I wouldn't disappoint him, not one bit.

I watched as the boy stripped out of his jeans. His legs were long and thin but, as I mentioned, his pants were skintight and he had trouble getting them off. Bending over to free his feet, his bubble butt presented itself to my devouring eyes. Framed by a pair of designer briefs, it looked simply delicious.

"Don't take those off," I told him.

"Don't take what off," he replied?

"Your shorts; leave them on. I want to see if I can get them down with my teeth," I said with anticipation rising.

"You know you can do that," the boy said. "You do it all the time."

He was right. After tracing the seams of his shorts with my tongue, and used it to play with the elastic band before I bit on it and tugged them away. What I revealed met my expectations and how I revealed it met his. In less time than I took to take them off we were leg locked and lying across the bed.

The kissing continued only now my kisses covered every inch of his body. It responded as expected, I saw to that. My fingers probed everywhere fingers can probe, as we continued to build toward serious sex. Finally I pulled away.

"Remind me," I told him, "why is it I only see you once a week?"

"That's all you want," he replied. "I'd marry you if you'd let me. Then you could have me every day."

"And why doesn't this happen," I wanted to know?

"You said it would interfere with your job, that your profession demands you stay free and that if it wasn't a cash transaction it wasn't going to happen," he whispered. "So shhhh, time is money and right now it's wasting."

He didn't need to shush me again; I closed my lips and used them to continue my assault on his silky smooth body. When his front side was done, I rolled him over and started anew.

Some guys are great in bed. Through practice or just natural skill, they just know what to do. They watch you, anticipating your needs, figuring out your desires. They make sure your satisfied in every way and that they're satisfied too. I'm like that. Again, I don't mean to brag but I'm one of the best. That's why I do what I do. I know that as well as I know my own name. I also know that I hate the fish. They're the guys who lay there all cold and dead and doing nothing but waiting soaking it in. By doing nothing, they force you to do everything. And, I might add, in my book they miss the boat. You need to convey what feels good so the guy doing you knows what to do. I really hate fish. Fish never let you know what they want; they're the deaf mutes of body language. They should be charged double for all the work they demand. This boy was speaking louder than necessary. Hell, he was practically shouting. I knew exactly what he wanted and he wanted it bad.

By the time we'd finished I was drained again. He was exhausted too. We both fell back on the bed and just laid there. With the exception of our breathing, nothing was hard anymore. I'd seen to that, and the boy had responded. Damn, he was good. I should be paying for him and he shouldn't be paying for anyone, I thought. I still didn't know why he was paying. I didn't know his name or anything else about him, but I knew he was good, damn good - almost as good as me!

Eventually the boy dragged himself from the bed and began to get dressed. He said he had to get going but wanted to know if we were going to go at it again next week. "Fuck yes," I had said, why wouldn't you want to do this kid? This week, next week, and the week after that... I'm not too sure why I wasn't with him all the time. If it really was my profession that got in the way, I needed to find something else. I could go back to school or drive a bus for that matter. This boy was worth getting out of the business, I thought. Then I got another thought, one that made much more sense. I should get him into the business. Two can make more than one and this kid was a natural. I'd have no trouble renting him out and together we could have the world by the tail. Speaking of tail, I'd have his more than once a week too.

The boy walked through the alcove and up to the toilet. I could hear his strong stream as it splashed in the bowl. He didn't bother to close the door, why should he? We had nothing to hide between us. I still might not know his name, but believe me, I know all I need to know. In fact, I considered, the only thing I don't know is how much I charge him. By rights, he should be charging me. I searched my mind trying to remember what I had charged the other tricks I'd entertained today. I couldn't remember getting paid.

Now, to anyone else these memory blanks might seem frightening, but for me they were normal. By now you must understand that my mind is different. I don't always know what I'm doing or why, don't always know with whom I'm doing it. Still, today had been one of my clearer days. I could remember every trick, the details of all our debauchery. Why couldn't I remember getting paid? I should be able to remember what I charged.

For a moment I considered giving the kid a pass. Shit, I

thought, he was good enough and I enjoyed it as much as he did. The boy was young and probably didn't have a lot of money anyway. I still couldn't figure out why he was buying it, but maybe today he shouldn't have to, maybe to day would be free. These were the things filling my mind - these and the continuing sound of his stream in the bowl - when I came to my senses. I'm not a charity, this is a profession. The boy would pay, he was used to it. Hell, I probably didn't have to tell him the price; if he was a regular he'd already know. I got up and began searching the room for my own pants.

I looked for quite awhile before finding them. They were stuffed between the bed and the wall so I couldn't see them at first. What I did see caused me alarm for the second time today. Richard's pants were still folded on the bed, his shoes and socks sat on the floor and his suit coat still hung from the chair. This was pretty creepy. I know that you know about my mind issues, but this just doesn't happen. I mean some times I can't remember things, some times I can't remember people. But I've already told you that this day had been pretty clear. I remembered Richard from this morning. I remembered David from the day before. I even was clinging to a distant memory of Robbie though it was fading. I probably could have remembered him better but we did lots of drugs you'll recall. My men tend to come and go, but they've never gone without their pants before.

I shrugged these thoughts off as I snugged my pants on, damn they were tight. I must be putting on weight though I couldn't recall eating all day. I remembered going to the lobby to get Richard some coffee, but I don't think I'd taken any food. It was such an effort sometimes. Why was I so clear on some things yet so blank on others? There were empty spots in my brain. My stomach was empty too. Maybe the boy who was still pissing was hungry too. I'd ask him if he wanted to grab a bite when he came out of the bathroom, I thought. Damn he could piss a long time.

After I finished struggling into my jeans and had tugged up the zipper, I realized that the sound of his stream had changed. Instead of the sound of piss hitting water it sounded like a downpour. He was really draining his lizard. I walked around the bed and into the alcove. The door was closed now and as I approached, it wasn't the sound of piss that I heard. Clearly the boy was taking a shower. Hadn't I just seen him dress? I was really getting confused now.

I knocked on the door. There wasn't an answer so I knocked again. I would have called out the boys name but I didn't know what it was. A regular customer and great sex not withstanding, I couldn't recall who he was and never figured out how to ask. To me he was just the boy and for some reason he was now in the shower. That was strange. Hadn't he just gotten dressed?

When the door didn't open after my third knock, I tried the knob and found it unlocked. Swinging it open, I peeked inside. The shower curtain was closed but I could still see the boy on the other side naked. Reaching out, I grasped the edge of the curtain and pulled it open. Imagine my surprise.

Inside the shower, the water washing down his body and the steam rising all around, it wasn't the boy at all. It was Richard. Richard Rassmussen, Attorney-at-Law!

"Wondered when you'd be back," he said stopping long enough to pick up the shampoo bottle and twist off its lid. "You been gone forever, I was afraid the hot water would run out before you returned."

Before I returned? I thought he was the one who was missing. I'd had three different tricks since I'd seen him last.

Where was the boy and how the hell did Richard get in here?

"You going to get in or should I just shut this off," he asked with his hand on the knob?

I looked down at the jeans I'd just managed to squeeze into. "No, I'm already dressed. I think I'll pass."

He replied, "Yea, I can see that. Do you have a fetish for my pants or what?"

Confused (aren't I always), I didn't know what he meant. It must have shown on my face. As he continued, he explained.

"My pants - all morning long you've been in and out of my blue jeans. I'm surprised they even fit."

His jeans? I looked down again and considered how tight I'd found them to be and how much trouble I'd had getting into them. So that explains that, I thought. They belong to Richard. And my clothes?

Not wanting to give my confusion away I thought quickly.

"You wanna wear mine," I asked?

"No way, Jose'," Richard said with a laugh. "I wouldn't be caught dead in a suit and tie. My friends would think I'd gone legit. Wore one once, to court, and the tie made me feel like I was getting strangled all day."

So, the suit out in the bedroom was mine. But, what about the wallet? Richard's wallet and his business cards were definitely in the suit pocket, my pocket. Was I ripping him off? And, for that matter, how did he practice law in a pair of skin tight Levi's, I wondered? He just said he'd only worn a suit to court once. Damn strange for an attorney if you ask me. It didn't make sense, so I asked him instead.

"So tell me," I asked genuinely wanting to know, "how does an attorney get by without wearing a suit?"

Richard began laughing. "An attorney? Me? Now that's a good one. I admit to being a professional man, but an attorney? My dear old Mom would be proud."

"But the business cards you were carrying? Richard Rassmussen, Attorney-at-Law", I prodded.

"Oh that," he answered as he stepped out of the shower and picked up a towel. "You gonna get on my ass for that again?"

"What again," I wanted to know?

"The wallet and the cards - I told you I'd give them back," he said.

"Tell me again."

He stopped drying himself with the towel. Dripping wet, a puddle forming on the floor at his feet, a naked Richard explained that he wasn't Richard at all. Apparently he'd taken the wallet and the business cards from someone else, one of his other "customers". I'd found them on him when we'd gotten undressed. And, it seems from what he told me, we had words. I accused him of being a thief. He tried to say he'd found them in the room after the "customer" had gone. I didn't believe him. He said he had promised to return them. Apparently I didn't believe him again. Eventually, I guess, I slipped the wallet and the business cards into the pocket of my own suit, having decided to get them back to their rightful owner myself. Richard, or at least the guy who I now knew wasn't Richard, had gotten angry. He had been pissed by my accusations that he was a thief. I'd told him to drop it and change the subject or I'd never hire him again.

So there you have it. He wasn't Richard Rassmussen, Attorney-at-Law. The wallet and business cards didn't belong to him. And, I wasn't the prostitute, he was. Life sure can get crazy, at least my life can. Not knowing what else to do, I did the only thing that made sense. I peeled his jeans down to my ankles and stood facing him in the confines of the small room.

"They were too tight for me anyway," I told him. Then I pulled him toward me, pushed on his shoulders and dropped him to his knees in front of me. I was getting a better picture of what was going on. He was the prostitute. It was he who was getting paid. Everything didn't make sense yet, it probably never would. But I knew now for certain that I had hired him and he should be servicing me.

"Well, get going," I demanded. "It's not going to suck it self!"

The man I now knew wasn't an attorney at all finished draining me for the fifth time today. Or was it the sixth? Seventh? Hell, I didn't know. I did know I must be the most overly sexed guy on the planet. That and I knew I must be rich. How the hell did I manage to afford all these hustlers? I tried to think, tried to search my befuddled mind. In the end, all I could remember was that I'd been famished when I walked through the door and his mouth was the only mouth that had been filled.

"You want to grab something to eat," I asked him as I wiped a drop of me off his chin?

"Breakfast? Sure, but do you have the time," he replied?

"Breakfast? I was thinking dinner would be more appropriate," I answered as he got to his feet.

"You're so funny," he laughed, "we just got out of bed. I thought that coffee you brought up was all you had time for. Weren't you going to be late for work?"

So, I was employed. I made a mental note of this new piece of information. That's how it works. You pick up a fact here; you pick up a fact there. Pretty soon a picture emerges and you get a better idea of what's going on. Employment explained where I was getting the money to hire all these hookers, if not the reason I was compelled to do so. Employment explained why I was up at the crack of dawn, even if it felt like the middle of the day. Employment explained the suit and the tie, which were mine. Now, I thought, if I only knew where I worked I'd be fine.

An alarm was going off. Like a slap in the face, the sound that it was making brought me out of my thoughts and back to reality, like that wasn't a joke. There was a naked man on his knees, on the floor at my feet. My pants, or rather his pants, were pulled down and my dick was dangling a few inches from his face. I didn't know who he was, didn't really know who I was. Clearly, neither of us was Richard Rassmussen, Attorney-at-Law. And, there was an alarm steadily sounding in the other room. Concentrate on that alarm, I told myself. It's the only thing that knows what it's doing here and right now it's trying to tell me something.

A Boner Book

CHAPTER FIVE
Friday

I stepped around the man who wasn't Richard. I still didn't know his real name, but I knew he was in my way, and I knew that I needed to get out to that alarm in the bedroom. It had to be silenced and it had to be silenced fast, before it was too late. I rushed out of the bathroom and blinked my eyes.

It was hard to see at first. My eyes seemed stuck together. My vision was foggy when I finally forced them open. My head hurt and my muscles were stiff and sore. The furniture had been rearranged, replaced was more like it. Nothing was the way it had been when I'd walked through the alcove and knocked on the door. Hell, the alcove wasn't even there now. I didn't know where I was, but I knew I was on a mission. I needed to shut that damn alarm clock off before it woke him up.

Him! I didn't know who he was, but I could see him still snoring in our bed. He was big. He was big as a bear. And like a bear, I just knew like I knew nothing else, you don't want to wake him when he's hibernating. Rather than fumbling for the button on the clock, I grabbed at the cord and snatched it from the wall. The alarm was silent and, for the moment at least, so was he.

I stood up. I was dizzy. Turning around, I retraced my steps and went back to the bathroom. No one was there on his knees. Nothing about the room looked remotely the same. The room still had a shower though, and I forced my aching body into it.

The water hit me like a ton of bricks. It's not that it had that much force, but my head hurt and even a fly landing on it would have seemed too much. I dropped my chin so the water would hit my neck and leave my throbbing skull alone. I spit. My spit came out red and salty. It was blood, my blood, and I watched it mix with the shower water as it swirled down the drain.

I stood there a really long time, waiting for the shower to take effect and sooth my aching. It didn't. Finally, I gave up. Twisting it off, I abandon the effort and stepped out of the tub careful not to slip. Across the wet tiles, I approached the mirror I found hanging above the sink. Did I dare look?

I did look. What I found looking back wasn't really that bad. I knew I'd seen worse. Sure, you'd think it was terrible. I know that. But I also knew what he could have done to me and in retrospect; this wasn't terrible, not terrible at all. My lip was split open and my left eye had a definite bluish-black dis-coloration. My eyes looked red and swollen, but that was prob-ably because I'd been crying. Nothing a little Max Factor couldn't take care of, I thought, and went about the business of getting ready for work.

How many times had I gone through this routine? I did-n't know. However, I did know that my lack of memory was the result of their having been so many, and not that I couldn't remember them. I remembered every time. I remembered every time he'd hit me, or pushed me, or thrown me down. I could recall his heavy work boots as they kicked my ribs and his callus covered hands as they dragged me by the hair. My memory was fresh and detailed. He was a drinker and a mean one. He said he loved me, but he made my life miserable. Yes, I could recall every sordid pain filled day of our pitiful relationship; I just couldn't remember why I didn't leave.

Dan was his name, though his friends called him Grunt. He was a U.S. Marine once, got the name there and it just stuck. The rest of whatever they taught him must have stuck too because he really identifies with that part of his life. He's as much a Marine now as he was then.

Dan is big, in every possible way. I can barely wrap my hands around his arms, or his biceps at least. He could pick me up and break me with no problem, and that is the problem. You see, Dan's got a temper. Now he'll tell you that the problem is me, that it's my fault; I cause him to get angry. I know that's not true. If anything, I work up a sweat trying to keep him from getting angry. Still, I love him.

I've loved Dan from the moment I first laid eyes on him. And, he loves me. At least he did. I kind of think he still does, it's just that he gets so damn angry. I'd like to get him to see a shrink but don't dare suggest it to him. Fuck man, can you imagine how pissed he'd be if I did? Oh, maybe you can't. I keep forgetting that you don't know him like I know him.

Maybe you'd get a better picture of the man if I told you a few things about our life together. We've been together almost twenty years you know. Hell yeah, twenty years, and in this day and age that's something. We ought to get a medal or something 'cause twenty years might as well be one hundred years in gay relationship's time. When I met Dan he was fresh out of the Marine Corps. He was trim and fit, not an inch of fat on him. These days he's had too much beer and it shows a little, but back then he was all muscle. I think he was doing like four hundred pushups each day or something. I don't know. But I know this, he looked good and it was love at first sight.

Dan was twenty-six, I was seventeen. His friends

teased him that he was robbing the cradle and things like that. He didn't care. He just wanted me. And he had me too. He got me for the first time in the back of his Dodge GTO. The car wasn't really an antique or anything, but Dan and his buddies really spruced it up. They'd restored it to factory fresh just off the showroom floor condition and it was sparkling. I thought I was like in the Presidential Suite or the penthouse or something. I was small and fit the back seat just fine, but Dan was really big. He really filled the passenger compartment and had trouble getting his pants off. I laughed at him, and it was kind of funny. Dan didn't laugh; he just clamped one of his big hands around my skinny little neck and told me to shut up - but in a nice way, sort of. Then he turned me over, shoved my face into the seat and (as he said at the time), fucked me like his bitch.

I've belonged to him ever since.

Within a week or two of meeting him, Dan insisted I move into his apartment. Who was I to argue? I'd been living on the streets in a way. Moving from friend's house to friend's house, I always had a place to stay. It's just that I didn't stay in one place very long and never in the same place twice. Once I moved in with Dan, things changed. From that point on in my life, I had a real home and a real man to come home to, in a manner of speaking. See I didn't really ever go anywhere so I wasn't really coming home to him; it was more like I was never gone. Oh, don't get me wrong, I go to work each day. Dan wouldn't have it any other way. We need the income and he says it's good for me to have some responsibility and besides, Dan says that if I'm at work then he knows where to come looking for me. He used to say that he knew I was safe at work but then one day he showed up and saw some of the guys who work with me. Like I'd really go out with any of them. And where did he think I'd get the time to go out anyway? So Dan doesn't trust me anymore at work. He calls three or four times every day. I know he's checking up on me and it makes me feel good to know he cares.

At first, like I told you, Dan's friends kidded him about robbing the cradle. My friends were different. My friends thought he was too old for me. But what did they know. After the first few times that he hit me, my friends said they were afraid for me. After he blackened my eye for the first time, and knocked out one of my teeth, well that's when my friends started insisting that I drop him, get away, and escape. Some of my friends even wanted me to call the police and have him arrested. I quit calling my friends instead. I couldn't stand their pressure and besides, Dan didn't want me hanging with them anymore.

You need to stop what you're thinking, just reign in your thoughts. You're starting to think the same way my friends thought and you know where that got them. I didn't need to leave Dan then and I don't need to leave him now. Besides, he never beat me like that again. Oh, the black eyes are still pretty common but he never, ever leaves any permanent evidence of his anger anymore. Plus, he paid for the dental work and the bridge to close the gap that was left when I lost my tooth. Dan's good like that, always looking out for me.

At first he didn't want to do the dental stuff. He was thinking that no one would want me with a big old hole in the front of my mouth. If I got it fixed, he'd explained, other guys would be coming on to me. Did I mention that Dan was terribly jealous? That's one of the ways that I know he loves me. He's just so damn afraid that someone else will come along and take me away. Stupid jerk, doesn't he know I'd never leave him. Besides, where would I go?

"Hey!" Dan's voice yelled out from the other room.

My body started shaking, my heart racing, as I hollered back, "In here! I'm just getting dressed."

"Just checking," he hollered back. "Don't leave without telling me goodbye. Don't do that again." Then, even though I wasn't in the room to see him, I knew that Dan rolled over, pulled the covers up to his chin and would soon fall back asleep. You see, Dan was a creature of habit and over the years my defenses had honed my ability to read him like a book. Dan hardly ever took me by surprise any more. If I was getting hit I knew in advance. If he was going to slap me around or kick my ass or anything, I knew it before he did. Hell, most of the time I brought it on myself so who would you expect to know first?

I looked back to the mirror and gingerly touched the open gash on my lip. It stung and I flinched back, gritting my teeth to the pain. Opening the medicine cabinet, I fumbled for some antiseptic and finally settled for the Listerine knowing it would clean the wound without leaving its own stain. A few passes with the Chapstick and it would appear that another cold sore had infected my mouth instead of a boyfriend infecting my life.

Dan's the man, I thought as I applied the Chapstick and picked up a cover stick. Motherfucker asshole! One of these days I'm going to quit covering his ass and just let people see what he's done to me; see what he's really like. But, not today. Today I get busy covering his crimes and fixing myself for work. I was most of the way done when I heard his voice behind me.

"Little miss pretty face I presume. How long you been using make-up, little girl?" His voice was filled with sarcasm and disdain. "Get the fuck over yourself," he continued. "And what the fuck was up with your alarm this morning."

"I tried to shut it off," I began to explain but the Grunt wasn't interested in hearing any explanations.

"Tried my ass," he yelled. "What don't you understand? I got to get my sleep and I've asked you and asked you to hold it down in the morning. What is it, don't you hear me? You got shit in your ears? I need to sleep and you don't seem to appreciate that fact!"

"Sorry hon," I tried to say, but mostly I just stammered.

"You do this one more morning and I'll kick your fucking teeth down your throat and without teeth, nobody will want you!"

The Grunt was still yelling, but I shut him off. He really did need his sleep, he worked second shift. And, I really did try to turn of the alarm as soon as I heard it. I should have flipped the switch as soon as I got out of bed. I wondered what I'd been thinking. It's not like I don't know how he is in the mornings. Then I remembered. Oh yeah, he kicked my ass last night, this morning all I could think of was getting into the bathroom and away from him.

I tried to remember why I got an ass kickin' last night. It seems to happen so often I can't always remember what I've done to deserve it. I thought long. I thought long and hard. I remembered he was pissed that his dinner was cold when he got home from work, that's how it started. It always has to start over something and last night it was his dinner. He had come home from work late and I should have put his dinner in the microwave, I should have kept it warm. It would have helped if he'd call and let me know he was going to be late, I'd told him and that pissed him off.

"Call? Call you? What do you think, I got nothing better

to do than call you're stupid ass? What is going on in that pea-sized brain of yours? I just told you I was working late. How the fuck do I call you when I'm working. I was too busy to come home and too busy to call and you were obviously too busy to care seeing as I came home to a fucked up cold pile of mush instead of the dinner I deserve."

"Sorry," was all I could say before he cut me off.

"Sorry? Aww, shut the fuck up before I give you some-thing to be sorry for. I'll rearrange your face so it'll be even uglier than it already is, you pitiful little shit. You know, some-times you're pretty - pretty useless!"

I wanted to cry, but I didn't. I wanted him to love me, but he didn't. What's wrong with me? He used to love me?

"I'm so sorry, baby," I tired again. "It won't happen again, I promise. It won't happen again."

The apology was my first mistake. That fucking bastard didn't deserve my spit much less my apology, but I gave it to him anyway. My second mistake was walking over close to him as I told him I was sorry. I guess I was going to offer him a hug; you know like kiss and make up. What I got instead was the reason I needed make-up today. Without warning his hand came up and caught me across the face. I'm not anywhere as big as The Grunt and his blow knocked me to the floor. He kicked me then dropped to his knee. The knee caught me in the stomach propelling my head up off the floor and directly into his fist. That's where I got the black eye.

He left me lying there and this morning, when I woke up, I left him lying there too. My plan had been to get dressed and slip out to work before he woke. It would have worked if I weren't so stupid to have left the alarm still on. Dan was right;

I didn't have the brains God gave a goose.

Dan could be charming. Like when we go out to eat, he always opens the door for me and holds out my chair. He knows what I like and Dan orders for me. If it doesn't come to the table just the way he knows I like it you can bet that the waiter will catch Hell.

Speaking of Hell, I don't want to give you the impression that my life is filled with it, 'cause it's not. Dan is very good to me, given all the trouble I've caused him. I mean, he didn't have to take me in. I was a seventeen-year-old, snot nosed street kid and he was an ex-Marine. I was a high school dropout and he had a college education. I weighed all of one hundred ten pounds and he could snap me in half with his little finger. I'll tell you what; I never slept in the streets again after meeting Dan. He totally took care of me. He gives me the roof over my head and the clothes on my body. Hell, he even cares enough that he picks out the clothes I'm to wear. Not too sexy, as if I'm really going to get anyone to look at me.

Dan, Dan, he's my man. Sometimes I'd like to kick his fucking teeth down his throat. Ha! Just kidding.

By now, I'd finished with the make up. Leaning back I took a long look at myself in the mirror. Not bad. Not bad at all, I considered. Not bad at all, given the beating I'd taken and the toll it had taken on my face. Now, I just looked like a faggot wearing makeup instead of a faggot wearing makeup who got his ass kicked last night. I put the tools of my transformation away in the drawer, clicked off the bathroom light and moved silently into his room.

There he was, a giant hunk of a man with his body pulled up in the fetal position on the bed. I really wanted to walk over to him, climb in beside him and make him feel good.

My arms around his big strong body, I'd give my own body over to him. I really wanted to surrender myself into his care. Problem was, he scared the shit out of me. That and he sometimes beat the shit out of me too.

I read in a book or a newspaper or somewhere that this lady whacked her husband after years of abuse and they didn't even charge her with murder. Maybe I saw it on television. I don't know, but I know that the cops or the prosecutors or the judge or someone said it was self defense from years of taking his shit. Lately I've been thinking I wish I knew who that cop or prosecutor or judge was so I could call him and ask him a few questions of my own. But then, I couldn't really hurt Dan. How could I do him wrong? You see, deep down inside I know he loves me. I know he wants what's best for me and I know that he doesn't want to be the big asshole he is to me. I've just got to be better and use my head. After all, Dan is the man, my man, now and forever.

I've only been with one other man since I met Dan and that one doesn't really count. It happened on my eighteenth birthday and I didn't really get with that guy, at least not willingly. Oh, he screwed me all right, but not with my permission. I always looked at it like rape. You can't blame the victim for the crime, right?

We were out celebrating. Like I told you, it was my birthday, you know. First we went to dinner and then to a club. Dan put away several beers and seemed to be having fun so I started having fun too. I was out on the dance floor for a long time and I guess that got him pissed. I should have seen it coming but I didn't. You know what they say; hindsight is better than foresight or something like that. Anyway, I guess he was standing there on the side of the dance floor just looking at me and watching who I was dancing with and stuff like that. I kind of knew what he was doing and I'd been careful to spread myself around. You know, I didn't dance with the same guy twice. Most of the time I'd been bouncing around in the middle of the floor and not dancing with anyone in particular. I'd rather have been dancing with Dan, but Dan didn't dance.

So, back to my story. After an hour or so I had to pee and walked off to the bathroom. In all honesty, I should have found Dan and asked him to go with me but you know how it is, hindsight again. The bathroom was small. There was only one toilet and one sink but there was also a urinal on the wall across from the toilet and when I walked it there was a guy pissing at that urinal. I really didn't pay him any attention. I was just going to relieve myself at the toilet but as I passed the guy pissing he kind of fell back. I guess he'd been drinking and had a little too much 'cause next thing I know, he's falling into my arms and it's pushing me down to the floor. That's where Dan comes in.

Actually, that's where Dan wanted to come in but couldn't. I told you the bathroom was small and now the guy who had been pissing at the urinal was laying on top me on the floor and blocking the door so it couldn't open. So Dan is outside pushing the door but it won't budge and the more he can't move it the more he gets pissed and pretty soon he's banging and banging the door into my side. Finally, I get up and get the guy on me up onto his feet so Dan can get the door open then BAM!

Dan's fist was so fast I didn't see it coming. I took the full blast of it straight in the nose. Instantly my nose exploded and everything was covered in blood, my blood! He accused me of fucking the guy who'd been pissing and it did look pretty bad. I mean the guy's dick was still hanging out and he was lying on top of me down on the floor and all. But I swear to God, nothing happened between us. At least it hadn't up to that point.

By this time Dan had transformed into The Grunt. He should have been slapping the urinal pissing drunk guy around but he was slapping me. He called me unfaithful and said how he couldn't trust me and stuff. He told me that since I obviously wanted it so bad that he was going to see to it that I got just what I deserved. With that, Dan ripped my clothes off, bent me over the side of the sink and made the other guy rape me.

"You want it," he yelled! "You want it up your cheap whoring ass, then take it! At least this time when his dick's up your ass your boyfriend will be watching."

"No Dan! No," I cried. I begged him to let me up. "Please, let's just go home." But Dan the Grunt wouldn't hear of it. The show had begun and he was in the director's chair. I was going to get fucked and the drunk guy with his dick hanging out was going to do it, that or die trying. Dan was going to make sure of it.

Well, to make a long story short the guy managed to get his dick in. I guess you could say he fucked me but I don't think he ejaculated. I'm not really sure but he was very drunk that and I was so fucking scared that I really don't remember. He worked his hips and pushed his thing in and out of me for five or ten minutes until Dan pulled him off and then did me himself. The sight of me getting piss fucked by the drunk guy must have turned him on 'cause Dan's dick was raging and he wasn't waiting for us to go home. He pounded me into the porcelain, so to speak. By the time he was finished with me, my ass was bleeding, my nose was bleeding, I was a fucked up mess.

I don't know what became of the drunk fuck piss person. He probably bolted from the bathroom as soon as he could. I'll bet he left while Dan was plugging my ass. I hated him so - I mean the drunken guy, not Dan. Thing is, I always thought the guy could have told someone. You know, like the bartender or the doorman or someone. He should have told someone that this kid was getting raped in the men's room but he didn't. He just split out of that bathroom and saved his ass while mine was being assaulted. Sometimes when I remember that night I just want to kill him.

That was the last time Dan let anyone put their thing up my butt. It wasn't the last time he put anything up there though. He fucked me with a bottle once. I pissed him off. Can't totally remember what I did to start it but I'm sure it was something bad 'cause he was really upset. He tried calling me throughout his shift, trying to tell me what I'd done but I wasn't home. The washing machine had broken down and knowing how he gets if the housework isn't done... well, I took the clothes out to the laundermat, that's all, I swear. So anyway, Dan comes home and accuses me of having an affair. Like I'm porking the neighbor while the clothes are spinning, but he wouldn't hear about it. Nothing I could say was making it better. In fact, the more I tried to explain, the more it pissed him off. Finally he just did it. Screaming something about the sex he perceived I'd just had in the laundromat he yanked down my pants and shoved his beer bottle up my ass.

"You fucking little whore," he kept yelling. "You want it up your ass, then take this!" He kept pushing that bottle in and out of my ass and I could feel the beer that was left inside as it splashed up into me. When he finished and let me go to the bathroom that beer came back out.

That was the only time Dan fucked me with a beer bottle but not the only time he used one for sex. He must have had a bad day or something cause he wasn't really drinking. Oh, he'd had a few beers by the time I walked in but he wasn't falling down drunk or anything. And, it's not like he's an alcoholic either. Dan has a rough job and I know I don't make life any easier for him; sometimes he just needs a beer to wind down.

Anyway, Dan's got this beer bottle in his hand when the argument starts. He wants sex and, to be quite honest, I just didn't feel like I was in the mood. As expected, Dan immediately assumes I don't want him because I've already had my fill of someone else. Honestly, he has nothing to worry about. I've told him over and over again that he's my man, that I don't want and don't ever have anyone else but he doesn't believe me. Instead, my protests piss him off and the next thing we're fighting. He's telling me we're going to have sex and I'm just trying to keep from getting slapped around. My hands are protecting my face and I'm not thinking clearly and who could? I mean, you're getting your face rearranged and you're supposed to think clearly? Not hardly.

Anyway, he's slapping my face and telling me that we're going to have sex and I, without thinking, tell him we're not. "Fuck you, you're drunk," were the words which accidentally slipped out of my yet to be swollen lips.

Now, you can do a lot of things to Dan. You can fuck up and screw up and generally piss him off. But, there is one thing you never do - not if you want to live, that is - never, ever, ever tell him "fuck you". It just isn't done, and I knew it wasn't done at the exact moment I'd done it. That's when my lips got swollen, and that's when the beer bottle came in, quite literally.

I found myself flat up against the wall, my shirt was in tatters and my pants had been yanked down. I wasn't fighting any more. Dan had broken the beer bottle and was pressing its sharp, jagged edge into my neck. He was a trained killer, having been in the Marines you know, and the bottle was pressed into my juggler vein right where it could do the most damage. While I stood there, face smashed into the wall and perfectly still, he entered me. I didn't say a word. He didn't either, at least not until he got done. He just silently fucked me, my body shoved into the wall and the bottle shoved into my neck. Finally he finished his deed, let himself slip out of me and let me slip down to the floor. That's when the bottle came back into play. He didn't cut my neck. That cut would show. No, Dan might give me a black eye or swollen lip or something I could easily cover with make-up but he wouldn't ever put a mark on me like the one he was about to - not where it would show.

Slowly, deliberately, with satisfaction in his pants and a smile on his lips, Dan used the jagged broken bottle to cut the cheeks of my ass. "D A N," that's what he carved. He put his name permanently onto my body and claimed me as his own. Later he told me that the scars were so ugly no one would want to fuck me. Sometimes he told me that if I ever had another boyfriend they wouldn't want to make love to me since the whole time they'd just be seeing his name. Once in awhile he'd tell me that the scars meant we'd be married forever and that seeing his name on my butt really turned him on. I hoped so. See, there wasn't anything I could do about the scars; they were as part of me now as my ass itself. And, I didn't plan on ever being with anyone else anyway. I was married to Dan in every way, and having his name on my ass became important to me. It was kind of like having a wedding ring. At times I'd reach back and trace the letters with my finger, and think of the man who put them there - my man!

Speaking of "my man", I brought my head down out of the clouds and began to wonder what he was up to right now. Had he gone back to sleep? I didn't think so. As he so often reminded me, he was a very light sleeper. It took him hours just to fall asleep, even if he was tired. Once asleep, the slightest thing could wake him up and if he woke up, he was up.

Pity the poor fool who wakes Dan up before he wants to get up, 'cause Dan's gonna be pissed. Thing is, I was usually the pitiful fool. Like this morning for instance, how the hell did I let that alarm clock go off? I knew better.

Glancing up at the mirror once more, I gently patted the make-up covering my darkened eye. I've gotten quite adept in the make-up department and this morning I'd been particularly adept at covering up last nights tell tale signs of Dan's abuse. I looked pretty good despite Dan's best efforts to the contrary. Yes Chad, I thought to myself, there are lots of guys who'd fucking fall all over themselves to get with you. You hot little fuck, you. Of course, I also thought, I'd never say these things out loud. Dan would simply kill me if he ever heard me say some of the things I've thought in my mind. And anyway, it's not like I'd ever really get with another man. Dan was all the man I needed and all the man I ever wanted. Besides, if I should ever forget that he was my man, Dan would surely make me remember.

Right now, I needed to remember to tell him how very sorry I was that I let the alarm go off again. I needed to kiss his hairy old ass a bit and make sure he wasn't going to dwell on this all day then kick my ass again when I got home from work. Where oh where can he be?

I left the bathroom and began to search the house. Dan wasn't in our bedroom. He'd thrown the comforter off when he got out of bed. Now, it was on the floor, as was the top sheet. Anxious as I was to find out where he'd gone, I just couldn't walk out of the room without picking the covers off the floor and making the bed. Dan would be on me if I didn't.

Down the hall I passed two unused rooms. Actually, we used them for storage; we just didn't use them as bedrooms. We didn't have that much furniture and probably didn't need a three bedroom home to begin with but Dan said there was no sense buying a house that didn't have at least three bedrooms 'cause no one would want to buy it from us when it came time to sell. Now we had two rooms we didn't need, neither of which I expected to find Dan in this morning, but I looked anyway. He wasn't there.

Downstairs I searched the kitchen and dining room and living room and halls but to no avail. That's when I started down the basement stairs.

Our basement is black. It's dank and smelly and I use every excuse I can find not to have to go down there. It creeps me out. Now, I found myself on the top step of a very rickety staircase, looking down into the depths of this gloomy place. I stood there a long moment wondering why we never got around to putting a light switch at the top of these stairs. Why must it be necessary to go all the way down in the dark before Edison's discovery illuminated the path? That's what I was thinking today, as I began my careful descent down the cellar stairs.

BAM!

The brightest light you can imagine exploded inside my skull. It came suddenly, without warning and knocked every other thought out of my head. There wasn't time to think, not a fraction of a second to consider what just happened. The only thing I knew was that I was still alive, but that could change quickly too. I was tumbling over and over down the stairs and into the basement. With each tumble I had enough time to anticipate the pain as another part of my body hit one of the wooden planks from which the stairs were constructed. First my head hit, and then an arm, then I could feel my feet come up behind me, tumble over my head and shoot forward in front of me down the stairs. My heels hit, my ass hit and then I was pitched forward, face forward toward the next plank. I didn't have time to really concentrate on the pain; it was more like I was just registering the fact that there would be pain. I guess that's how the brain works. You take note of the things as they happen so you can be sure to feel them later when you remember them in detail. Right now I didn't have time to remember to put out my hands or break my fall. I just kept tumbling and tumbling and tumbling down the longest flight of stupid stairs you can imagine. Finally, at the bottom, I crumpled into a pitiful little heap on the cold damp concrete.

"There, that ought to get you to remember to shut the damn alarm off in the morning." It was Dan's voice, coming at me from on top of the stairs. He must have come up behind me. Opening my eyes I could see him standing up there, way up at the top of the stairs. I could see his big construction boots and just knew I'd find the imprint that one of them left on my head if I could get to a mirror and look back there. I was afraid of what else I might find if I got to that mirror.

"I said I was sorry," I heard my pitiful plea.

"Yeah, now you are," he snorted back. "Next time you'll be careful with the alarm clock and the stairs. Both of them can make you hurt."

Now you'll think I'm crazy and perhaps I am, but at that precise moment, lying on the basement floor and looking up those creepy stairs to see him towering over me - well, all I could think was how big he was, how strong and how much I loved him. Sure he could be an asshole sometimes, but he was my asshole and I knew that he could protect me from just about everything except myself. I gotta work on protecting me from me, I thought, Dan's got everything else covered.

I watched him turn and walk away from the stairwell.

When he'd gotten four or five feet away he turned again and came back. Reaching the top of the stairs he stopped took hold of the door and slammed it shut. I lay in total darkness waiting for him to just go away.

There in the dark, on that damp basement floor, my mind was wandering. Half of me wanted to just get up, get my stuff and walk out the door. You know what I'm saying? Leave! That half of me was thinking that if I just walked out the door and out of Dan's life I might be able to get my own life together and be free. The other half of me wanted to know what the fuck I thought I was going to do with my freedom. Who was going to take care of me? Who was going to make sure I was all right. Dan was an asshole sometimes but the truth was that sometimes I deserved it. That and sometimes he just couldn't help himself.

After lying there thinking for several minutes I picked myself up and slowly climbed the steps back into the kitchen. There, in the bright light I examined my body and took stock of the damages. There were some pretty good bruises but these were mostly on my arms and legs and they wouldn't show. There were no broken bones, no chipped teeth, and nothing gushing blood. I guess I'd be all right.

I was fairly certain that Dan was no longer at home. No doubt he'd left for work himself, just after he slammed the basement door on me. Knowing him the way I do, he probably figured I'd either get up and get to work or just die there in the basement. Either way, no one would be waking him up or pissing him off or anything. Silently moving through the house, I made my way back upstairs to our bedroom. Like I said, I was certain that Dan had gone but better safe than sorry.

You can't always be sure why someone is mad at you. I mean most of the time, if I knew what I was doing to make him mad I wouldn't be doing it. A lot of times you do things that you don't even think about and if one of them makes him mad how the hell are you supposed to know it? As I reached our room and found a clean shirt to wear, I made a mental note to be better. If I could only keep my wits about me and pay attention to what was going on, I was sure I could please Dan and make him love me.

My thoughts were on Dan all day at work. At lunch I stopped off and picked up some fresh pasta. There was a little store near my job that sold the best fresh pasta you could want. Pasta being Dan's favorite, fresh pasta should do the trick. After work I'd pick up some flowers, maybe a movie. Tonight was going to be our night and tonight would make up for the things I'd done. Thinking and planning all this made the day simply fly by and before I knew it the end of my shift came.

As planned, I stopped at the florist and got flowers. I picked out red and white carnations. They were simple and plain and cheap. Roses were fifteen dollars per dozen. For the same money I got two dozen carnations with greens and still had enough to put a single rose in the middle of the bouquet. I picked out a pink rose. Pink is the color of true love you know. Amid the bright red and white carnations, the pink is going to stand out. For a second I'd considered getting a yellow rose. Yellow would have really jumped at you from all that red and white. But yellow is the color of cowards.

Usually Dan gets home before me but only 'cause my work is farther away. I have to take two busses and still walk several blocks. So, I half expected to find him waiting for me when I finally made it home. He wasn't. Figuring he must be working late or maybe he stopped off for a beer with his buddies or something, I set about putting Dan's dinner together. But before I began work on the dinner, I placed his flowers in the center of the dining room table. Just in case he comes home before I'm finished cooking, I thought, at least he'll see flowers.

Back in the kitchen I set about opening cans and boiling water. Yeah, yeah, I know what you're thinking; fresh pasta then sauce from cans. Actually, the sauce was still going to be mine. I make it with tomato paste and canned tomatoes and lots of onions, mushrooms and spices so it's nothing like store bought and certainly doesn't taste like it came from a can. I'm quite proud of it. Served over pasta cooked just so, it's literally delicious. The pasta has to be slightly underdone to be good. Since Dan still hadn't arrived, I thought I'd better make it really underdone. That way, when he did get home, I could just drop it back in the boiling water for a few minutes and finished it off. To stop it's cooking and put it on hold, I placed it into a strainer and ran it under cold water. That's when I heard them.

To be honest, I didn't know it was them at first. I didn't even know that it was Dan. The sounds I heard sounded muffled and I didn't know what they were. Clearly they were coming from upstairs. Thinking I was still alone in the house, I climbed the stairs to find out what was making the noises. At the top of the stairs the noises were louder but no more distinct. I still couldn't tell what they were, but I know knew where they were coming from. At the door to one of the spare bedrooms I stopped. Placing my ear to the door and holding my breath I listened. This was one of the rooms we used for storage. The noises I heard were coming from inside this room and while I still couldn't comprehend what they were, I did know they came from a person.

He was grunting or something, and I could hear boxes being shifted and moved around. I may not be the sharpest tool in the shed, but I knew that something was wrong. There was someone going through our stuff; a thief! Now my heart was pounding. Oh fuck, I wished that Dan was here. I wish he'd come home and take care of this for me. I'm thinking what would Dan do when it hits me. I probably should have just run to a phone and called the police but at that moment it wasn't a phone that came into my head. See, when I considered what would Dan do, he wouldn't call the police. No, what Dan would do - what I did - was grab a weapon.

In a hall closet between that storage room and our bedroom was all Dan's sporting equipment. I'm not going to tell you all the junk he had in that closet 'cause my heart was pounding then and it's pounding now just telling you about it. Suffice it to say, I picked up the biggest Louisville slugger I could wrap my fingers around and returned to that storage room door ready for battle. My heart really was pounding. It was so loud you'd think the burglar would have heard it but he didn't. I could still hear him grunting as he picked up and moved things around, searching for stuff to steal. As my fingers tightened around the doorknob, my other hand tightened its grip on the bat.

Shock!

That's what it was; shock. I'm still in shock, sort of. You see, when I finally got up my nerve and opened the door it wasn't a thief moving boxes that confronted me. It was Dan! He'd been home all the time. And he wasn't grunting because he was moving heavy boxes, he wasn't searching for stuff to steal. He was face down on the floor, pants to his ankles his big white ass waving in the air. Under him and also face down to the floor, a pimple faced, skinny, teenage grease ball was getting shit fucked by my man!

Now, if you were the judge or a member of the jury or even one of the cops who were eventually called; you'd be thinking that I should have been thinking but I wasn't. I didn't take time to think. I didn't take time to consider my options.

Heck, I didn't even take time to look at the punk's face to see if he was someone we knew. All I knew was that he shouldn't be down doing Dan; not right in front of me anyway.

Slam!

The bat hit Dan first. I didn't really want to hit him, not then at least. Right then I wanted to kill the kid with Dan's dick up his ass but Dan's ass was in the way. They both would be dead if that first swing had connected with Dan's head; but it didn't. Instead, the Louisville slugger slammed into the place where it would do the least damage. I smashed Dan's ass.

Let me tell you, if you ever want to kill the mood for sex, just slug someone with a baseball bat. The fucking sure screeched to a halt. Dan was off that punk fuck and up in my face before I could pull the bat back for a second swing. He grabbed at it, pulled it out of my hands and dropped it to the floor. Immediately my hands flew up and began pounding him over and over on his face, his chest, anywhere I could connect. When Dan managed to grab one of my hands I'd pull it to my face and bit him as hard as I could. When Dan let go, I'd scratch at him with my nails before striking him again.

Dan's bigger and stronger and if I hadn't been so crazed he could have just pinned me and that would be that; but it wasn't. The fight went on for several minutes. It only ended when I quit fighting and I only quit fighting when I finally looked past Dan and saw that skinny little faggot I'd caught him fucking. The kid had picked up my bat but he wasn't using it to defend Dan or even protect himself. He was holding the bat in front of himself, covering his dick so I couldn't see. I kid you not, that's what he was doing. This kid is all shy or something and he's hiding his shit behind the baseball bat I was just going to kill him with. What a dumb fuck, I thought, and immediately began laughing.

I know you're not a psychologist or anything, but you surely can see what happened. The anger and rage that was exploding inside of me was suddenly replaced by laughter. As strange as it sounds, that's what ended the fight. The sheer sight of that little asshole covering his even smaller prick up so I couldn't see was just too much to take. I roared.

I really couldn't stop laughing. It was just like the anger when I swung the bat; the same emotional rage that fueled my fistfight with The Grunt. I laughed and laughed and laughed, all the while watching Dan take the bat from the kid and help get him dressed. I laughed harder when I finally saw what the kid had been hiding. His dick was skinnier than he was. This was what Dan chose over me? As Dan led him out of the room, down the stairs and out of the door I just kept on laughing. I really couldn't stop. The thought of that little shit taking my place made me laugh. His skinny little dick made me laugh. The thought of this kid holding up under Dan's onslaught really brought the chuckles out of me. Dan would break this kid in half. One good punch and the kid wouldn't be hiding that skinny dick; he wouldn't even be hiding the black eye he'd receive. Fuck, if Dan ever beat on this boy he'd be blind. A picture of that pimply puke, skinny shit hiding his dick with one hand and his black eye with the other popped into my mind and I laughed some more.

I was still laughing when Dan came back into the storage room. That calmed me down. If he thought he was coming back to finish me off he had another thought coming. My hand shot to the bat as I came off the floor to face him. His hands shot up to cover his face and apparently shield himself from me. That made me laugh too. What the fuck; here was this big, strong motherfucker and what was he doing? He was shitting his pants for fear I was going to hit him.

"That's it," I heard myself say as I stopped laughing and dropped the bat. "It's over, you're history. I'm not going to hit you and guess what you stupid shit. You're not going to hit me ever again either."

I couldn't believe the words coming from my mouth. Like where did I get brave? I'd never spoken to Dan like this before but what the hell; I'd never felt as empowered as I felt now either.

"I'm leaving you Dan. You can fuck that skinny kid or anyone else you care too, but you can't fuck me; not anymore. You can slap him and hit him and beat the fuck out of that puke if you want; but you're not going to touch me ever again." Then, mustering more strength than I knew I possessed, I shoved past The Grunt standing in my way and raced to the bedroom.

Dan followed, but he was too late to stop me from pulling the suitcase down from the closet shelf. Frantically pulling shirts and jeans from dresser drawers, I was packing that bag when he walked in the door. I braced for a fight but it didn't come. Instead, Dan sat his big stinking ass down on the floor beside me and began to cry. I couldn't believe it. I'd never seen him cry before and it unnerved me big time. He could have done just about anything else to convince me to stay; and it wouldn't have worked. But crying? Holy fuck, that just tore me apart. It was too hard to watch him bawl like a baby right there in front of me. Soon, I was sobbing too.

We sat sobbing for some time. Wrapped in each others arms, neither one of us saying a word, we simply cried together. It was a bonding thing between us. When at last we'd cried all the tears we could, I stood up and pulling his arm to follow, led him down the stairs and into the dining room. There on the table, two dozen red and white carnations surrounded a single pink rose. I let Dan think about those flowers while I returned to the kitchen, boiled the water and finished the pasta.

Sometime later, after we'd eaten and after I'd done the dishes we talked. Dan told me how very sorry he was and how he'd never ever cheat on me again. He also told me how this whole thing could have been avoided if I'd been a little more caring and more considerate of him. I hoped he was really sorry though I didn't know for sure. Also, I didn't know if it were true that he was never ever going to cheat on me again. I did know that it was probably my own fault and that there were things I could do to make it better. I also knew that certain things were definitely not going to change. Dan was Dan and I knew he loved me. But he didn't entirely know how to love me; at least not in the way I wanted. If I had balls, I thought, I'd leave his sick fucking ass and find someone new. But those thoughts faded as he took me in his arms and all but crushed me as he carried me back up the stairs and to bed.

There would be many more nights in our relationship, but this night was one to remember. Dan made love to me.

Long after Dan was asleep I lay there still, thinking. My lip started to throb. I let myself fall into that piece of pain and considered that it probably had throbbed all day but the emotions covered it up. Funny how a thing like being angry worked the same way as a tube of cover stick. Being really fucking angry worked much better. Basically, I'd forgotten all my pain all day and only now let it return. Now I was exhausted. I reached up and touched my lip. It was clearly still swollen; I could feel the split skin. I wondered if Dan had ever hit that skinny puke kid. Had his lip ever been split? I hated that little fucker and vowed to crack him with a bat should the occasion ever arise. Then, letting my hand slip down under the waistband of my shorts, I traced Dan's name with my finger. He was my man! That skinny fuck knew it now, I thought. And, he better never forget, if he knew what was good for him. With that thought, I closed my eyes and fell into sleep.

A Boner Book

CHAPTER SIX
Saturday

It was another one of those mornings when I woke before the alarm went off. I woke a full ten minutes before the alarm and I felt cheated. Damned if I'm going to move, I thought. I was entitled to those minutes and determined to make the most of them.

I never closed my eyes but watched those minutes go by on the clock. For a while I was trying to anticipate the precise moment when the L.E.D. light would blink and one minute would become the next. That simple exercise was lost however, as the memories of the yesterday flooded my mind.

There'd be no repeat of the mistakes I made. This morning I hit the switch long before the alarm goes off. To be sure, today I'm going to pull the entire fucking plug out of the wall. I'll slip silently away from Dan and let him get his full fucking fill of sleep. Instinctively my hand moved up and touched my lip. It didn't seem so swollen this morning and I couldn't feel the skin split at all. Perhaps I'd get by without make-up, I thought.

I also thought about the things Dan said to me after dinner. I knew with absolute certainty that life was going to be different from now on, his anger and his violent behaviors were going to stop. Still, I kept watching that clock; preparing to rip the cord out of the socket so as not to take any chances. After all, last night wasn't the first night that Dan had told me those things.

My mind wandered back to a slap, a punch, an ashtray thrown at my head. There were stitches and scars and a burn mark! I'd forgotten about the burn mark; forgotten how The Grunt held me down, pinned to the floor, while he rubbed his cigarette out on the inside of my thigh. I'd so hated him at the time. Still, he apologized. He said life would be different. We both promised to work harder.

Buzzzzzzz!

Shit! How the fuck stupid am I, no wonder I make him punch me. While my mind was wandering it hadn't been watching the alarm clock. Now, instead of having its plug pulled out it was blaring is wake up message like a fire alarm. Shit! Oh, Shit! My hand shot out from beneath the blankets and my fingers curled around the cord. I yanked that cord so hard the clock flew off the nightstand and half way across the room. At least now it was silent. So was I. I lay there barely breathing, hoping against hope that Dan had slept through that awful racket.

I lay there five minutes, or was it ten? I just know I did-n't move for a really long time. Finally, when I was convinced that he was still deep in slumber, I rolled over slowly and faced my fears.

His back was to me and the blankets were drawn high on his neck. Deeply sleeping, I watched the rhythm tic move-ment his breathing made. He looked so small now. Hardly the big bad man he thought he was.

I studied him, or at least what little part of him I could see under those blankets. I traced the contour of his neck, considered the lobe of his ear, and how his long blonde hair curled around it.

My eyes opened wide!

One thought flooded my mind and I was instantly awake and breathing hard. Dan didn't have blond hair. Dan's hair was short and dark and this man wasn't him.

Holy shit! I tried to calm down. Here it was, another day. And here I was, my mind crisp and clear and remembering every single detail. Now it's unusual when I have a day like yesterday; when I wake up and have a full understanding of who I'm with and what he's like. But this morning was different. This was the worst. This morning I remembered it all; literally everything!

I remembered Dan and the skinny puke punk he fucked. I remembered him kicking me down the stairs and busting my lips as well as my chops. That wasn't all that strange. What was strange was that I could remember more. I knew about David and how much he loved me; knew about Robbie and Richard and fuck, I knew them all. I could even recall the scores without names, and the hundreds before.

Hate! Hate! Fucking I hate mornings like this! These are the worst; I thought and began to shiver. You don't want to remember as much as I could. It freaks you out to know that nothing is going to change. Sure, I'll wake up with a new boyfriend each morning, but the fact that I'll wake up with a new boyfriend each morning - that will never change. Like the Flying Dutchman or Brigadoon, it will keep on happening day after day after day.

I began to cry.

I didn't cry long loud sobs. I was still very aware that my boyfriend was sleeping beside me. I wasn't ready or anxious to wake him and discover the new and exciting life I'd face today. Right now I just wanted to lay here and feel the warm drops of my own tears as they slowly slid down my cheeks. It's comforting somehow, when it's just you and your tears.

I cried for Richard and Robbie and Dan. I cried for David and Maurice. Then I remembered that I'd almost forgotten Maurice and I cried some more. Mostly, I cried for myself. How did I trap myself here?

Several minutes later, still crying, I realized that I didn't really know where "here" was. Sure, I could describe the room and take some clues, but today at least, I had no idea where I was. I had no idea who I was with. The man in my bed might be an asshole or he could be my soul mate. Today could be wonderful or a kick in the ass. I just didn't know. Now, I suppose most of you could say the same thing on any given morning but in my case it was different. After all, when was the last time you got kicked down the stairs? For that matter, when was the last time your boyfriend threw a state dinner in your honor. This morning, for whatever reason, I could answer both of those questions. I just couldn't tell you who the man I woke up with was.

Glancing across the bed I knew that he was my boyfriend, I just didn't know which boyfriend and I didn't want to wake him up to find out. That's when it hit me. Today was Saturday. I didn't have to work today. Nothing compelled me to get out of bed so I rolled over and went back to sleep.

POST-SCRIPT

Let me ask you a question. What would you do if you woke up each morning with a different boyfriend?

Hey readers it's me, Chadwick White. By now you've heard my story. Well, to be perfectly correct, you've heard five of my stories. There have been so many more. For reasons I may never understand, I wake up each morning with a different boyfriend.

I'm really quite happy to have found a publisher willing to let me tell my stories, or at least these five. I wanted to tell you the sixth story, the story of what I discovered when I finally woke up and got out of bed on Saturday morning. That story really wraps up this whole thing.

Unfortunately, Saturday's story had to be truncated in this book. I simply ran out of space. The good news is that my publisher has granted me a sequel. In my next book I promise to finish that sixth story. I'll tell you what answers I found and the the decisions I made that Saturday, decisions which finally brought sense to my crazy, crazy life.

Until you have the chance to read that sequel I'll heave you with the question I asked at the start of this page: What would you do if you woke up each morning with a different boyfriend?

PUBLISHER'S STATEMENT

Even as *Out of Body* goes to print, we're working to produce it's sequel. As Chad promised, that second book will wrap things up and bring some answers to his otherwise disjointed life. In the mean time, we can't help wondering how our readers answered Chad's last question. What would you do?

To find out, we've decided to give Chad his own website. It's a place where you can log in and read a few more of Chad's stories. Most importantly, the website will allow you (our readers) to answer his question and let us know what you would do if you came to realize that each morning you were waking up with a different boyfriend. How would you react? What would you do to help yourself remember from day to day? Would you even want to remember?

The website is free, all we ask is that you decide to post an answer or one of your own stories, give us the rights to publish it when we publish the second book about Chadwick White. Until then, please visit Chad at http://www.ChadwickWhite.com.

About the Author

Ron Ehemann lives in Chicago, Illinois. While he has been published in numerous magazines and newspapers, *Out of Body* is his first novel.

Ron likes to say he's surfed the cultural wave. Born into an "Ozzie and Harriet" family, he was active in the Boy Scouts, Sons of the American Legion and his church youth group. Life changed drastically with the death of his mother at a very young age. When Ron's father re-mairred he suddenly acquired six siblings and a "Brady Bunch" lifestyle.

Ron left for Northern Illinois University in 1968 and as we all know, 1969 was the "Summer of Love." Viet Nam followed and with it, the author's development as a peace activist. Though he earned the distinction of being the first student to drop out of ROTC at NIU, he managed to avoid the draft in an unusual way; Ron became a police officer.

In 1972, at the start of the Gay Rights Movement, the author moved to Chicago to attend law school and immediately became active in the community. As it's Assistant Editor, the author helped found and establish Gay Chicago Magazine, which continues in publication today.

Ron Ehemann graduated from Chicago Kent College of Law and immediately entered private practice as Chicago's first openly gay attorney. Virtually overnight his practice grew to include many of that city's gay bars, organizations and businesses. Prolific writing found him published in numerous magazines and newspapers around the nation during this time. He appeared on a number of radio and television shows and was eventually profiled in Newsweek Magazine.

In 1980, Ron established his relationship with Chuck Renslow, a prominent businessman and political heavyweight in Chicago's gay community. Now writing for Chuck's newspaper, GayLife, Ron was also becoming heavily involved in politics. He co-founded the Organization to Promote Equality Now (O.P.E.N.), the first gay political action committee in Illinois. Together with Renslow, Ron also helped establish what would eventually become the Prairie State Democratic Club. Under the administration of Mayor Jane Byrne, the author was appointed to Chicago's Commission on Human Rights. Though a subsequent administration failed to confirm that appointment, Ron still holds the distinction of being the first openly gay man to be appointed to a political office in Illinois.

After several years as a litigator, the author left his private practice of law and devoted himself to Chuck Renslow's varied business enterprises including Manscountry baths, the Chicago Eagle leather bar and International Mr. Leather.

For the past twenty-five years, the author has been a prominent member of the "Renslow Family", a communal group of men and women, straight and gay people who have bonded for life. Ron is raising two boys, ages seven and eleven and lives with them in a very large home which he shares with

Chuck and the rest of the Renslow Family, along with several dogs, cats, turtles, fish and what ever other animals his boys bring home.

www.ingramcontent.com/pod-product-compliance
Lightning Source LLC
Chambersburg PA
CBHW071224260626
47162CB00004B/1413